The Ombú Tree

The
Ombú
Tree

ELISE DALLEMAGNE-COOKSON

1998

FITHIAN PRESS

SANTA BARBARA, CALIFORNIA

for Lucía

my friend

and for

Pierre Edmond Dallemagne

my son

in loving memory

Contents

∼

…There is the world
dimensional
for those untwisted by
The love of things
irreconcilable…

Anonymous

The Ombú Tree

~ Part I ~
Argentina!

But I'll tell no more of the sufferings sore,

Of our long-drawn tale of woes;

At last at the end of all our ills,

We saw far off a range of hills,

And not long after we trod once more

The land where the ombú grows

Martín Fierro, by José Hernández

≈

HEN Diana walked into the bus station in Rosario at six A.M. in the Argentine spring of 1962, the first thing she saw was the bold headline on the morning newspaper: "¡REVOLUCIÓN!"

She stood before the newsstand clutching her little son's hand, and her heart skipped several beats. Her hand shook as she bought a copy of the paper, realizing she was all alone in the middle of *another* South American revolution, barely able to speak the language, with two-year-old Philip by her side, and only ten dollars worth of pesos in her pocket.

The Rosario bus station was a miserable place, almost deserted and still littered with the debris of the previous day's travelers. Diana shivered in her lightweight, well-tailored gray wool suit. The dawn she had greeted with hope an hour before now appeared bleak and without a friend.

The newspaper reported many things she did not understand. There were two factions; one called the *Azules*, which meant the blues, and the other the *Colorados*, the reds. They were fighting each other in the streets of Buenos Aires, as well as in the military base outside the city. And the fighting was spreading to other military bases scattered throughout the country. It was very confusing, but what was clear were the few lines at the end of the news story stating that since late afternoon of the previous day the armed forces had been stopping all trucks and buses, commandeering them for their own use.

A fist closed upon her guts. Our trucks! Had they taken our trucks? What was happening to Michael? A man like him would not have given up without a fight.

Passengers for the Las Rosas bus began arriving at the station, and while everyone carried newspapers, no one seemed concerned about the blazing headline story.

"Will the bus leave?" Diana asked one passenger, pointing to the newspaper headlines. The man looked puzzled, probably not understanding her broken Spanish.

So she asked another passenger, who shrugged. "Why not?" But she did not believe it until the bus actually pulled out of the station.

Michael and Diana a piece of land. A much smaller piece than what the former government had promised, but one they could reasonably afford. A *campo*, as a small farm is called in Argentina.

"No one, but no one, escapes the port of Buenos Aires without paying. Bribes, at the very least. You're a genius," Mr. Cobbens, a middle-aged Belgian entrepreneur who had befriended them, told Michael.

"No. I just wore them down, that's all."

"But what I really don't understand," Cobbens had continued, "is how you, a foreigner, and an Englishman at that, ever talked the Consejo Agrario Nacional into selling you a campo. Land that was confiscated during Perón's land reform program to be sold to local Italian tenant farmers."

They had been approaching Las Rosas, 250 kilometers north of Buenos Aires in the Province of Santa Fe, where the campo lay. Cobbens had offered to drive them there to take a brief look at their farm. "Then it *is* a good piece of land?" Michael had asked.

"Sure. This part of the country is probably the most fertile in all of Argentina. Smack right in the center of the *Pampa Húmeda*. And I'll also wager that your campo has been fought over for years. I'll bet every farmer in the area has, at one time or another, tried to get his hands on it. So watch out. You're going to have to deal with some strong feelings among the local people."

When they arrived at the campo, Michael had been so excited that Cobbens had hardly stopped his car before Michael jumped out, scrambled over the sagging gate and rushed forward up the weed-choked road to inspect his new farm. But Diana had found herself numb, unable to move, crushed by a sudden and completely unexpected feeling of being utterly alone, lost in a flat, silent, featureless land where there was no place to hide. As he stood next to her under the roof of blue that is a pampa sky, Cobbens told her, "I think you're crazy."

Maybe so, she had thought to herself. *But we will not fail.*

That same day Cobbens had returned them to Buenos Aires, telling Michael, "Well, you're either the world's greatest optimist, or the world's biggest fool."

"I prefer to think optimist," Michael had laughed.

"Well," Cobbens had smiled, "if love is all you need to succeed, I guess you'll make it. You two actually radiate it. Fill up the whole place with it. Wherever you go.

"It can actually make a guy feel uncomfortable," he whispered

the formerly dull, placid faces of the women gleamed with warm smiles like sunshine breaking through winter skies. They had made it safely home from the big city. Their peculiar Spanish dialect called Castellano was so rapid Diana could barely understand what they were saying and could not catch even a passing comment on the revolution from any of them.

After the bus rattled to a halt at the end of the town's single paved street at one o'clock in the afternoon the passengers scattered quickly, leaving Diana standing alone with Philip in front of a shut-tered café. The bus driver waited by the door, his motor running, watching her solicitously. After a few minutes she answered his in-quiring stare in halting Spanish: "Someone is to meet me here."

Thus assured, he climbed back aboard his old machine now car-rying only a handful of passengers. He cranked the roller above his head and turned his bus around, heading it back up the paved street toward a place called S. Jorge.

Dusty roads surrounded her. All empty. A silence lay over the town as though its inhabitants were holding their breaths. The sun burned white in a sapphire sky, and Diana could smell the spring, fresh and new, in the soft breezes caressing the town, making its de-serted streets and its shuttered storefronts appear even more aban-doned than they were. Leftovers from another season, another time.

The buildings were mostly singled-storied, and there were cracks in the mildewed concrete. In some places the cement had fallen off, exposing the rough, hand-hewn brick underneath. Some of the squared-off roofs were decorated with columns and open bal-ustrades of aging masonry, like Roman ruins, among which weeds sprouted.

There was a single horse tied to a hitching post in front of one of the shuttered stores. A gaucho hurried out of the building and leapt upon this horse, and in so doing brought Las Rosas back from the dead. The fierce-looking man wore loose-fitting royal blue trousers that were tight at the ankles and a long-sleeved bright or-ange shirt. The brim of his black felt sombrero was turned back from his eyes and a silk scarf the same color as his trousers was tied around his neck. As he galloped away, Diana noticed a large dagger thrust through his wide belt.

After fifteen more interminable minutes on the street corner outside the shuttered café, Diana decided to go looking for Michael. Or at least try to find some other means of transportation to their campo.

what I intended to do here—he suddenly stood up and told me, 'All right, old boy. Go on. Take your pickup and your trucks and get out of here. But I'd stick to the back roads if I were you.'"

"What did he say when you told him you were going to farm here?"

"I don't think he believed me. At first, anyway. He couldn't understand why someone like me would want to milk cows."

They climbed into the pickup and Michael started the engine. As they turned the corner onto the main street of Las Rosas, Diana glimpsed faces that appeared at the murky windows of the café behind the bus stop. In some houses, curtains were boldly parted as they drove by. Feeling almost giddy now that Michael was once again by her side, she wanted to wave at the wondering populace.

Turning onto the highway, Michael said softly, almost to himself, "You know that officer really seemed to regret leaving England. He talked about his years in the Royal Navy as though they were the best ones of his life...."

Then he continued with his story: "It was dark by the time the drivers reloaded the trucks and the roadblock lifted for us. By this time the Navy men thought I had to be some very important person, and they waved good-bye, all smiles, as we passed through."

"Did you see any fighting?"

"No. The streets were completely deserted. But I could hear sporadic gunfire, and the shooting came from the direction of the presidential palace. The Casa Rosada. A few small fighter planes were circling overhead, and then I recognized the rumble of tanks over cobblestones. It's a sound you never forget.

"After that I let the trucks take the lead since the drivers knew the roads where we would least likely be stopped."

About a quarter of a mile north of Las Rosas Michael turned left off the highway onto a red dirt road the color of dried blood where a crooked wooden sign indicated the way to Iturraspe. The road had been scraped and graded so often, and with such ferocity, it seemed the very heart of the pampa had been reached and laid open, wounded and bleeding. On the other hand, jade-green pastures and freshly ploughed fields of black earth surrounded the travelers like a luxuriant rug, bright and new, carpeting the land all the way to the horizon.

They were silent for a while, accustoming themselves to the sudden rocking motion of the pickup upon the rutted road. When he was able to continue, Michael went on, "After Buenos Aires, we

H E couldn't understand why someone like me would want to milk cows...."

Nor still can I, Diana mused as they drove along the red and rutted high road to their destination. How had it come to be that a dancer in the New York City Ballet and a London engineer were now speeding their way to a small farm in the Southern Hemisphere, on the other side of the world, thousands of miles from either one of their homelands? To a farm that hadn't been inhabited since the days of Perón's land reform? And that was twenty years ago. What's more, it probably had not been lived on or worked for many years before that because Perón bought up only abandoned *estancias* for his program.

Nine months before, December in London, Michael had flung open the door of their little flat to announce, "We're leaving!"

He was grinning like a man who has just made a powerful decision and was thoroughly pleased with the extent of his courage. Though it was only four P.M. it was already dark outside, the fog thick, and the dim lamplight in the flat reflected in his green eyes like prisms.

"What do you mean?" Diana carefully asked.

"We're going to Argentina where at this time of year one is standing in the sun! Breathing fresh air. Riding horses! Harvesting wheat. Corn. Sunflowers. Even milking cows if you want."

Their English collie, Alex, barked wildly, automatically responding to the joy his master had brought in the door with him from the foggy London night.

Diana frowned. "*Argentina?*" She tried to calm their dog by forcing it to lie down by the side of Michael's favorite old brown leather easy chair.

"Yes!"

"Why Argentina?"

He collapsed in his chair and took Philip onto his lap, staring silently up at her for a long moment.

"Have you ever been there?" she persisted.

"No...but my mother once had an Argentine friend when we lived in Paris. She used to tell me stories when I was a child. Of the

poured them each a glass. Settling down onto their couch, she tucked her legs under her and said, "Yes, Michael. My father, too, had dreams. Of farming. But my mother would never let him go. She always ridiculed him as being impractical. And kept him chained to that small town where I grew up and to that secure accountant's job he held for forty years. In the last years of his life how much he yearned for a tree farm in Maine, at least! He tried to convince her that raising trees would not require anything of her. They could just sit back and watch them grow as they grew old themselves. But she would have nothing of it. Deep down I think she was scared."

Diana refilled her glass, then told him: "But I am not scared." She stood up. "Yes, Michael, I will go with you. I left the theater for you. But that's not really true. I was beginning to hate it when I first saw you at the ballet here. No. Don't worry. I didn't leave the theater for you. I just left the people in it...."

She needed to refill her glass once more and told him again: "No, darling, I am not scared like my mother was. I will become a pioneer like my great-grandmother!" she laughed. "Yes, I will go with you. Because I love you. You see, I really have no other choice."

He came over to her, pulled her to his side and led her gently off to bed. He did not make love to her, but rather held her like a beloved companion in his arms all through the night.

In the morning over breakfast he announced: "In the war I learned that with land, my family will never go hungry."

That day he quit his job and began buying books on agronomy, while Diana started taking Spanish lessons.

Michael slowed down. "This is the road to our *campo*," he said, making a right off the red clay highway onto a smaller dirt road. "And this is where our land begins."

Nine months after his decision in London, he had his farm and a new profession. The immigration officer hadn't hesitated when Michael told him what he intended to do in Argentina. He stamped his papers: *"Profesión: Ingeniero Agrónomo."* "Profession: Agricultural Engineer."

Diana's husband was a man of action. Power and purpose.

cheetah, looking back at them, barking at them to join him, run with him, share in his joy. And Diana called out, "I know! I know! Oh, God, do I know!"

"I had to wake up the man who owns the kennel," Michael explained. "He didn't like that one bit. All the dogs howling. He must have thought I was a burglar, because he met me with a gun. But I just grabbed Alex and raced like mad to catch up with the trucks."

"*Thank you.* Oh, thank you, darling." She kissed him long on the lips and hugged him hard, ignoring the two truck drivers.

The unloading was completed about four P.M. The men wished them luck—but without much conviction—as Michael paid them. They looked at Michael and Diana in a way that made it clear they did not believe these young foreigners were actually going to farm this land and live in that old house, or *casco*, as they called it.

"It can't even be called a casco," one of them said as he climbed back into the cabin of his truck. "It's just an old dormitory for *peones*. And it hasn't been lived in for years."

As Diana watched the trucks diminish in size in the distance, crawling one behind the other up toward the high road, she said, "You know, I think they think we're crazy."

"Of course," Michael laughed again. "But what do they know?"

After a short while Michael decided he'd better run back to Las Rosas. "I'll get us some supper before the stores close. Will you be all right, or do you want to come?" he asked Diana.

"No. I'll stay. But take Philip with you. I need to do a little exploring."

Once alone, Diana sat down for a moment to rest on one of the half-open crates strewn in front of the casco. The immense silence of the land struck her again with fear. Only the shrill warning cry of a tero tero bird somewhere far away punctuated the stillness.

"I think you're crazy," Cobbens' words echoed in her mind like a mocking chorus. She rose and faced the land, shouting into the silence, "*But we will not fail!*" she promised herself for the hundredth time.

She returned to the casco: a long, low building of unfinished handmade brick. Bordered by squat, sturdy trees with black trunks and thick glossy green foliage on one side, and giant eucalyptus on the other, it sat snuggled into an almost imperceptible curve in the land, framed by the forest behind. So old and weather-beaten was the rugged building that the color of its bricks blended into the bark of the trees surrounding it like a resourceful animal which has found the secret of adaptation through camouflage.

There were four large doors opening onto a long verandah, and there were two more of these doors at each end of this verandah. It was more like a gallery than an ordinary porch, such was its length. Built in the shape of a rectangle, the building resembled a crude fort. Its tin roof, littered with dead leaves and branches, lay almost flat between two brick walls rising five feet higher than the roof itself. It looked as though someone had once decided to add a second story to the building but had succeeded only in adding to the original two side walls.

As Diana unlatched the first of the heavy, broad-planked, barn-like doors and looked around, she realized that there was no communication between one room and the other. The only light within the room came from a single western window, long and narrow, set into the bare brick wall, its window panes missing. And it was fitted with five iron bars as thick as a man's finger, placed only four inches apart. The sun was now falling behind the trees, and the daylight filtering through the barred windows cast an ominous shadow onto the rough brick floor, like that of a prison cell.

She found a similar barred window in each of the other rooms. The walls were darkened with smoke and age, and the high beamed ceilings had long ago turned as black as charred timber. Indeed, in one room she discovered the remains of a fire someone had once made in the center of the room, directly on the brick floor. Each time she pushed open a door she could hear a few frightened mice scurrying up into the rafters overhead. At the far corner of the gallery she found a room even more cavernous than the others. Inside was another door that took considerable effort to dislodge and lift over the uneven brick floor. It led to a room much smaller than the others and filled with even more gloom.

Two inside wooden panels covered the window bars, and only a little light filtered through a crack in one of the old boards, creating grotesque shapes on the wall facing her. Looking about, she realized they were the shapes of large sharp hooks embedded in the rafters, like those used in slaughterhouses for hanging carcasses.

As she stood in the doorway of this room that had been closed to the world and its sunlight for so many years, she had a sure sense of having taken the wrong turn, of having intruded upon something strange and strong that belonged to the past.

She hurried out to find Alex and with him discovered the orchard behind the casco where orange trees were blooming. Their

"Good. Perhaps we can use him."

"I don't think so. He looks strange. Wild...."

"We shall see. Come," he told her. "There is much to be done. And the first thing is water. We shall need a new pump for the well. In the meantime we can get our water from the windmill in the *monte*."

"Where?"

"The monte. The woods. There." He pointed to the forest behind them. "Any grouping of trees here, no matter how large, is called a monte. There's a windmill there and, I'm told, it still works, although it's in bad shape."

"I didn't see one."

"Yes. Look." He put his hands on her shoulders and turned her toward the setting sun, which by now was burning out like a hot coal behind the forest.

"You can just about make it out. Over there," he pointed. "To the right, almost at the edge of the woods. You can see it behind that row of trees, just as they start out of the monte. There are some blades missing."

All she could see at first was the setting sunlight, the color of rubies, streaking across the far horizon. But soon she could see a crippled windmill, silhouetted against this red sky, turning lazily in the gentle breeze of the oncoming night.

They walked back to the casco, where Michael spread his purchases down on one of the crates. "How everyone stared!" he exclaimed. "When I told them where I was going to live, the people appeared surprised but said nothing."

"No comment at all?"

"None. They just stared at me."

"That's funny."

"They seemed shocked. That's all. Maybe Cobbens was right. The locals have been wanting to buy this place themselves. And now that a foreigner has arrived to take over, I think they're just a bit pissed off."

They hurried before night fell to feed Philip and find his bed and theirs among the crates. Then they unpacked the stove and attached the cylinder of propane that Michael had brought back from Las Rosas. Diana forgot her fear. She even began to laugh as she and Michael watched Philip playing with Alex, rolling in the grass.

"Strange thing, though," Michael said. "I overheard someone ask a shopkeeper if this wasn't the campo that was haunted."

"Well," he sighed, "Monsieur Lambert, her husband, finally took her back to her estancia. But it was too late, I was told. She died soon after."

"Of what?"

"I don't know. And we couldn't ask Lambert. He left Argentina immediately after her death, and from then on no one was allowed to mention Argentina in his presence again."

"Where was her estancia?"

"South of Buenos Aires, I believe."

He glanced again at the ombú. "My God, how homesick she must have been. I often found her sitting by the window of her apartment, playing her Argentine songs on her guitar as though her heart would break. Tears would be streaming down her face, and she would be staring out as she played, seeing, I'm sure, her pampas. Not the gray stone buildings of Paris."

After supper Philip clapped his hands when he saw his bed put together, climbed in, and fell gratefully asleep. His eyes were already closed as Diana softly kissed him goodnight.

Diana and Michael then walked over hand-in-hand for a closer look at the ombú tree, Alex running ahead of them. Looking up the broad brown trunk into the massive black-green foliage, Diana could hear the evening wind murmuring among the leaves, like many voices whispering.

"You know," Michael marveled, "its seeds travel with the wind until finally finding the place they need to settle down and take root. Once strong and sturdy, nothing can kill an ombú. Neither the wild winds which sweep up from Tierra del Fuego and howl across the land, nor fire. The great prairie fires of earlier times which destroyed everything in their paths spared only the ombú because its limbs cannot burn."

The land on which the ombú stood was slightly higher than that which surrounded it, its great roots lifting up the earth from the surrounding flat terrain. From there Diana could see much of their campo, though there was almost no light at all left from the day. Just its remains streaked low over the land before her. Gazing out over the grassland sea stretching all the way to the eastern horizon, she saw a few groves of trees far in the distance—other montes than "the place across the way"—scattered in the twilight on the edge of the horizon.

She stretched out her arm and pointed: "Don't those montes remind you of ships at sea?"

*C*HE following morning they could get nothing but military marches on their transistor radio, interrupted every fifteen minutes by a recorded announcement from Army General Juan Carlos Onganía. The General assured the people of Argentina that all was well in the land, that he was firmly in charge of the situation, and that they had no reason to fear.

At eight A.M. the martial music suddenly stopped, and a triumphant Onganía told the people that his group, the *Azules*, had won. Guido, as president of the Senate, will act as the constitutional substitute for the deposed President Frondizi, but he, Onganía, as Chief of the Army, would be in charge of the peace of the nation.

"The revolution is over," he proclaimed. "All business," he ordered, "shall return to normal. And the perpetrators of this outrage, the traitors within the loyal Argentine Army, the glorious Argentine Navy, and the valiant Argentine Air Force will be properly punished."

His announcement was immediately followed by the throbbing, melancholy music of a classical Argentine tango. The military marches were over, and nothing more was said about the revolution.

"Good!" Michael exclaimed, relieved. "That means it's back to business as usual."

"But what was it all about?" Diana wondered.

"Power. Power struggles in the military. They are the ones who really run this country, along with the oligarchy—the big land owners. Always have and probably always will. The so-called democratically elected governments are just for show. And now that the banks are reopened I must return to Buenos Aires tomorrow to get our title of property from the Consejo for collateral."

"When will you leave?"

"Tomorrow."

"*What*? We just got here!"

"We have no time to lose. We need a loan if we are to start planting pastures *now*. Begin building our dairy. Planting the winter wheat this summer. I plan to put all the land to the south in wheat this year!"

her to come behind the counter to help herself.

The more bold among the customers smiled, especially at Philip. "*¡Qué lindo!* What a beautiful child!" they said, but not without some difficulty. Some offered him an apple, helping themselves from a barrel by the front door, or gave him hard candy from a basket on the counter.

He gravely accepted these gifts, his silver gray eyes lowered, his blond head bent with shyness. And then turned them over to his mother. Diana thanked them. "*¡Gracias! ¡Gracias! Muchas gracias.*"

One store was empty when she came in, but as she ordered she felt the darkened room fill with people. When she glanced around there were many faces staring back at her. They had come not to buy, but simply to witness her performance. She felt as though she were on a stage, without benefit of a script. She smiled at her somber audience, wanting to tell them, "Hello, it's nice to be here. And, yes, this is my son. I know his face doesn't look very pretty, but I appreciate your saying it is." She decided that the next time she came to Las Rosas, she would wear a dress like the other women. Perhaps it was her tight-fitting jeans that were attracting much of the attention.

Diana's next stop was the bakery. Unlike the general stores that were dark and had sawdust on the floors, the bakery was full of light. A busy place. Several horse-drawn wagons, old cars, and pickups were parked and double-parked outside, being loaded with large wicker baskets full of bread. Diana hesitated inside the door, feeling very much like an outsider but enjoying the delectable odors of freshly baked French bread, shaped in the form of large rolls and stacked in big laundry baskets behind the counter. As soon as the baker brought out a supply from his ovens, a full basket was snatched up by a waiting customer and carried out to his wagon or truck.

The local women were stuffing one or two of these rolls into their shopping bags, while the men in from the countryside were filling large white muslin sacks, which they slung over their shoulders, carrying them away to their assorted vehicles or strapping them onto the backs of their horses.

All the fixtures in the bakery were made of light oak: the counter, walls, and floor. Even the single display case was made of oak, bleached by years of scrubbing. There were only a few dozen sugar cookies inside this case, as well as some pastries that appeared to have been there for some time. It was obviously only bread that the people came for.

"Yes." It was as though she had committed some kind of crime. "But if you don't have any—"

"Sure!"

And he reached over to his butchering block table and slapped an entire beef liver down on the marble. As she started, wondering what Alex would do with it, he plunked down a large heart as well.

"Enough?"

"Oh, yes. Thank you."

"Nothing more?"

"No. No. But thank you so much."

Resigned, shrugging his mountainous shoulders, he proceeded to wrap the meat up in newspaper for her without even weighing it.

As he was doing so, she noticed Philip looking at two pretty little dark-eyed girls peeking out from the curtain at the back of the butcher shop. When Diana smiled at them, they quickly disappeared.

Turning back to the butcher, she asked, "How much?"

Several other customers, all men, were watching and waiting for his answer. He shook his massive, melon-shaped head and said, "Nothing."

"But—" Diana tried to object.

"Oh, it's so little," he told her. "It's not worth charging you."

"I'm sorry...."

The man's face softened. "It's all right. You will come back. You will be a good customer," he almost smiled.

Once she had stepped out the door, the men inside the shop exploded with laughter. She heard one of them exclaim, "Gringos! They're all the same! They don't know how to eat!"

Diana's last stop was the gas station, where she picked up two additional cylinders of propane for her stove. As the attendant was putting them into the back of the pickup, she found the courage to venture, "It seems that the revolution is over."

"Oh, yes!" he quickly replied.

"So soon?"

"Yes. They try not to kill anybody, Señora."

"I see...." Searching for more information, she asked as innocently as she could, "What will happen now?"

"Nothing," he answered matter-of-factly. "These things never change anything for us. You don't have to worry. The Army will probably exile the insurrectionists. The *Colorados*, you know, who took part in it. They might even execute them. But I doubt it."

DIANA was so busy during the week that followed she rarely stopped to worry about being alone with a small child with no way of getting help if misfortune should befall either one of them. Every day she arose earlier than the preceding morning, hoping to accomplish more. She swept down the rafters and scrubbed the walls and floors, unpacked the crates, and, though she had seldom wielded a hammer, fashioned a crude pantry in the kitchen from one of these crates. She experimented with sacks of cement and chalk Michael had left her until she had the correct mixture to fill the holes in the walls.

Early in the morning and in the evening twilight, she took long walks with Philip and Alex, getting acquainted with her land. In the evenings she sat under the ombú with them and played on Michael's guitar, until Philip was ready for sleep.

Together, mother, boy, and dog learned the habits of the field mouse and the prairie dog and observed how the hare could leap high in the air and bound across the fields, scattering the tiny birds who made their nests in the wild grasses. They discovered that a big iguana lived inside the drainpipe on the side of the casco where a great willow stood. This old tree tormented Alex for it contained several deep holes in its broad trunk high up out of his reach, which Diana suspected were opossum dens. They happened upon a hairy armadillo and witnessed his getaway as he dug himself a hole in the ground with amazing speed. Once Philip surprised his mother with a pheasant's egg. Although he didn't speak as yet, Philip laughed often, and with delight. He was happy.

His doctor in London had told Diana, yes, he was late in speaking but assured her it had nothing to do with his cleft palate. It was not unusual, especially for a boy who was an only child, his every wish anticipated by a doting mother. "He will speak one day," the doctor assured her, "when he has to. Don't worry. But in the meantime try to ignore him from time to time so he is forced to speak." But when she did so, Philip cried with rage at her callousness. If she continued to ignore him, these tears would lapse into sobs of profound sorrow at her hardheartedness. Michael was not worried. Rather, he reproached her for making his son unhappy, repeating

found nothing. All was still and silent again, as if the peace of the night had never been violated.

These tumultuous outcries were repeated every night, sometimes three or four times. The cause remained a mystery, until one afternoon when Diana found Philip in the orchard, playing under one of the old quince trees, cooing to himself contentedly as he pushed pieces of wood over the earth, pretending they were ships at sea, or trucks upon the road. As she bent down to gather him into her arms, she glanced up into the maze of branches that twisted skyward. There, curled up on the lowest limb, directly above him, was the largest cat she had ever seen. It was completely orange, with absolutely no other markings. Some kind of pampa bobcat. It appeared to be sleeping and did not stir as she slowly backed away.

She took Philip into the casco and returned alone with the shotgun. It still had not moved. Its body was muscular, its paws immense. The cat opened its orange eyes and looked directly into hers, and as it tensed on the limb, pointed, sharp talons curved like an eagle's grew from its powerful paws. Diana raised the shotgun. The cat continued to stare hypnotically. Malevolently, like a warning. Diana hesitated and the cat sprang away from her, down from the tree and out across the field.

The terrible noises on the roof at night stopped.

Soon after, the white horses of the monte appeared to Diana. They came cautiously, almost to the edge of the monte, heads held high, muscles taut. Barely visible, they watched: standing like statues in the twinkling sunlight filtering through the foliage. They also surprised Alex, and he barked wildly at them, but still they did not move. Diana quieted him and then moved slowly to the fence so as not to frighten them, speaking to them in soft tones.

They came often after that, usually in the early evening. She would continue to play with Philip, shouting and laughing so these guardians of the monte would become familiar with the sound of her voice. She was determined to further explore her monte and wanted their approval. Sometimes they watched her for as long as a half-hour, and then, without warning, they would turn sharply and gallop away into the depths of the forest.

One afternoon while Philip was napping Diana left Alex to watch over him. She had seen the horses drinking from the decrepit water tank on the far edge of the monte and decided she could risk a brief trip into the monte. As she crept deeper and deeper into the woods, the more calm she became. A feeling of joy and peace came

Diana found herself visiting the monte as often as she could, drawn by a magnetism she couldn't quite understand. One day, near the center of the forest, she came upon a thick hedge of laurel almost fifteen feet high. When she discovered a place to squeeze through, she entered an open area where the grass grew low. The only trees were fruit trees, strategically planted in groups of twos, threes, even fours. It was an orchard. A great orchard that made the one behind the casco look like a kitchen garden for servants.

She recognized peach trees, pear, apricot, and plum, along with many varieties of citrus, including kumquat, mandarin, and lime. Guava, perhaps, low-lying figs, pomegranate, and, standing tall in the far corners, were broad-leafed avocados and mangoes.

Why? By whom? For whom was this enchanted forest created? This orchard with its incredible variety of delicate fruits from around the world?

As soon as Michael returned, and she had transportation, she would ask people in Las Rosas about the monte. There had to be some reason that would explain the kind of peculiar serenity she felt there—different from any feeling she had ever experienced. It was like the peace of an abandoned cemetery, long forgotten, where the trees are tall, and wildflowers cover the fallen tombstones. Perhaps, she mused, here's where the real ghosts are, not "across the way." And there had to be not one or two ghosts, but several. Not common ghosts, either, she was sure, but spirits of consequence who must be happy with their afterlife.

Diana began taking Philip with her into the monte, leaving Alex outside to guard the casco. She was afraid he would frighten the horses, although she had yet to meet them during her walks. Alex did not protest being left behind; in fact, he let it be known that he had no intention of ever entering the monte, that he wanted nothing to do with it, and would wait on the other side of the fence for Diana's and Philip's return.

One day Diana found a group of giant eucalyptus planted in a circle and close enough to resemble a virgin forest, where little sunlight filters down through the tops of the trees. After the harshness of the naked sun in her open fields, the light within this circle was restful to the eyes. It descended in shafts so well defined, separate, and apart from the shadowy light into which they beamed, Philip tried to grasp them with both hands. They were sparkling, unbending beams of sky dust, containing all sorts of living things. Diana sat in the shadow of one of these ancient trees, watching her son as

BEFORE dawn the following morning Diana was startled by the distant sound of a tractor plowing the field across from the ombú, until she remembered that the Consejo had rented out that parcel of their land to a local farmer before the Consejo had sold it to them. He was plowing in the dark with only the headlights of his tractor to show him the way! He must be very industrious or late getting in his crop, reasoned Diana, and she realized she, too, would have to get up earlier each day if she were to accomplish all that had to be done.

As she waited for the first light, she planned how she was going to transform the casco into a home, imagining what their farm would eventually look like. Michael would turn the black-brown earth into rich green fields, scientifically selected and seeded pastures populated with pure-bred cows endowed with enormous udders. Calves would be frolicking about on the manicured greenery. There would be horses, too, and Philip would learn to ride like a gaucho. People would come from all over Argentina to admire their modern, automated dairy, which Michael would design and build. Although neither she nor he knew how to milk a cow, nor had even seen one except from the other side of a fence, she was not worried. She was certain that Michael, who exuded confidence as surely as a lamp gives off light, was capable of doing anything he chose to do. And he would teach her.

The sight and sound of the farmer ploughing across from the ombú kept Diana company for the rest of the week. By four A.M. each morning she could see the headlights of his tractor coming up her road, and he worked without stopping until eleven A.M. Then he would make himself a fire upon which he cooked his meat and, once nourished, would rest under one of the trees that came out of the monte, stretching in single file across the top of his field. After his siesta he would climb back onto his machine and work until one hour after sunset, when he would unhitch his plow and lumber off down the road in his tractor.

He never entered the casco or even set foot in the clearing in front of the house. Once a day, however, he would come to the edge of the clearing, clap his hands by way of calling to her, and ask

corn, and Diana was alone again. The field had been plowed, disked, raked, seeded, and now lay bare and brown but full of hope, while she had finished cleaning and painting three rooms of the casco, filling in the holes and cracks in the brick walls.

She tried to remove the bars from the windows, even though Michael had warned her: "Perhaps someday you might be grateful for them." She attacked these bars with a hacksaw, thinking, I am willing to do anything, but I cannot live in a prison. After ten minutes of concerted sawing, though, without even making a dent in them, she realized she was doing something wrong. Michael could be right.

Once she decided to keep the bars, she was determined to make the windows the most beautiful the casco had ever known. When Michael returned, she would screen them, replace the broken panes, paint the hungry, neglected wooden frames and shutters. She would cover them with yards of voile and bright linens or brocades. The ugly bars would be hidden.

Alex announced the arrival of their first caller long before he had chugged to a halt before the casco. The man remained in his ancient Chrysler as Alex continued barking wildly at him, leaping up the side of the car. When she had calmed him down, her visitor got out of his car and, with a nervous grin, quickly shook her hand. "Good day, Señora. I am your neighbor to the north. I am Señor Montoya."

A tall, rough-looking man of about forty-five, he was dressed in comfortable, baggy tweeds and the knee-high rubber boots of a working farmer. His face needed a shave or a thorough cleaning, and his sharp, dark eyes darted everywhere at once.

"Is he savage?" he inquired, looking apprehensively at Alex.

"Oh, no! Not at all!" laughed Diana. "He's just so excited to see someone. My goodness! 'Savage' Never. Not poor Alex. We call him Alexander the Great, but he's more like Alexander the Puny."

Señor Montoya gave her a questioning look. Then his eyes swept over the casco, and he said, "You're living in *there*?"

"Yes, of course."

"How can you?" he demanded.

"Oh, but I've been doing a lot of cleaning. Had to practically shovel the dirt out. The amount of spiders alone!"

"I can imagine," he murmured.

"Won't you come in and see what I've already done?"

wooden crates from Sweden marked *Alfa-Laval*, "it could be different. But we'll see. We'll see."

"Is there a farm close by where I could buy milk? Until we get our own cows, of course."

He thought for a moment. "You could try the Berratos. They sell some milk to the cheese factory. It's the campo next to mine."

"Thank you. I will visit them."

"We just keep one cow. *Para el café*. All the rest is beef, wheat, and corn. Some sunflowers."

Once again Diana invited the man into the casco for a cup of coffee, walking briskly into the kitchen, expecting him to follow. He took off his cap and clutched it tightly in his hands. Standing in the doorway, he glanced furtively about the room and asked what the deep-freezer was for and the washing machine and dryer.

"Hot water, too," he murmured, when Diana explained what the gas heater was for. He sat down carefully on the edge of a kitchen chair. "You know how to *operate* all these things?"

The modern electrical appliances suddenly appeared ludicrous to Diana, sparkling white and brand new in the primitively constructed room of uneven walls and floor. "Yes. Of course," Diana smiled, but at the same time felt she should somehow apologize for their existence.

It was late in the afternoon. The sun had already passed the window, and she felt a chill in the room. She pulled her cardigan close as she sat down at the table facing Señor Montoya. He watched her shiver and then exclaimed, "Well! *Madre de Dios*! Where did you farm before?"

"In the United States," she lied.

"The United States?"

"Yes."

"Of North America?"

"Yes."

"Oh.... You're having a lot of trouble up there with all your black people, aren't you?"

"A bit, I suppose."

"Well, we have a peaceful country here. You won't have to worry. No. Nothing like that. We have a few *Negroes*, but that's different. No blacks. No. We don't have any blacks in this country. You have nothing to worry about."

"What about the revolution?"

"That was nothing. No. You don't have to worry about things

stare at her for a moment, as though struggling with the desire to tell her something. But in the end all he said was, *"Adiós.* My wife wants to meet you. I'll soon bring her over."

"Oh, please do!"

As Diana watched his car bounce away like a rubber ball over her road, now deeply rutted as a result of a few rains and the passage of the tenant farmer's tractor, she wondered at this strange visit. Why had the man appeared so nervous, especially inside the house? He didn't act like someone who was jealous of their land, or even of their machinery. Still, she was grateful for his visit. Someone had, at last, acknowledged her presence in the countryside.

"Do you know that we are living on the site of the original homestead of one of the greatest estancias in all Argentina? In fact, it was once so extensive it was actually called *Estancia La Argentina*. I'm sorry to have done this to you but—"

"I understand."

"I'm proud of you."

"It wasn't so bad," she answered, grateful for his praise. "I was only frightened at night, and these past few days I've been looking for you all the time—"

"Yes," he stopped her and looked around the room, seeing it for the first time. "You've done a great job."

"Thank you," she smiled. "Go on, though. Please tell me."

Michael got up and began to pace the room in his usual manner: clasping and unclasping his hands behind his back. He told her he had found the original deed in the archives dating back almost 400 years to when the King of Spain rewarded a *grandee* called Casilda for his services with a large grant of land in the Argentine. Later, this territory was incorporated into the Province of Santa Fe, and Casilda's land alone made up almost three-fourths of the province. The original grandee never set foot in Argentina, nor did his sons, or his grandsons. But one of his great-grandsons did.

"He was politely exiled, I assume, from the court of Spain, and chose this very site, right here where we are now living, as the center of his empire."

"I knew there had to have been a reason—"

"Yes," Michael rushed on, "and as the years went by, the land was divided up, but passed only into the hands of Casilda's descendants. Never leaving the family. Each member was given a share of the land as he came of age."

"I wonder why, then…why aren't there more buildings?"

"Well, because first of all, few of the landowners ever actually lived on the land or worked it. It was wild then, and there were too many Indians. Most of the Casildas preferred to live in Buenos Aires, Córdoba, or Santa Fe. But their real income always came from this land which they would visit perhaps once or twice a year for the *cuenta*, as they called it. And they still call it that. The reckoning. That time of the year when they count how many head of cattle they have."

From the documents in the archives Michael had been able to piece together the history of the last three generations of Casildas. The grandfather of the last owner of their land was a supporter of

The old ironwood gate, which Diana could never budge, opened easily for Michael. The air inside the forest was cool and fresh, and the perfume of lilacs surrounded them as they hurried up the shadowy road, with Philip close behind. Alex stayed by the gate.

"I haven't seen any house here," Diana told him.

"I know. It burned down. But there should be something left. Let's look over this way," and he left the road. "Near the windmill. It couldn't have been too far from water."

They made their way through the underbrush between the trees until they came to a hedge of laurel similar to the one that enclosed the great orchard. It was difficult to slip through the thick bushes, but once on the other side, they found themselves inside a large grassy clearing. There they saw the two white horses grazing among the ruins of the house for which they were searching. Looking up at them, the proud animals tensed for a long moment before retreating slowly toward the windmill.

"They know me by now," Diana explained.

Michael began to search about, pulling a clump of myrtle away from a mound of earth about six feet high. The soil fell away easily, exposing a wall of bricks which looked new in comparison to those they had just found near the ombú. Elsewhere, jasmine covered another wall where they found pieces of hand-painted Spanish tiles. Oleander bushes were scattered about the clearing, as well as croton plants with exotic leaves, some dark red with black and white stripes, others green and white with yellow dots. Rose bushes, long since gone wild, entangled themselves everywhere among the ruins.

As he continued to search, Michael told Diana, "Dragonetti, at the Consejo, remembers this house well. He told me it was one of the finest in the land. Don Pedro used only the best materials for his daughter, who was all he had left after he lost his wife. Alicia died soon after his daughter was born."

As they continued to search among the ruins, Diana began to experience a sense of personal loss, as though the house had been built for her instead of for the daughter of the last of a long line of Spanish grandees. "Did the daughter have any children?"

"Apparently not. When she died, the land was abandoned for a long time, and that was why Perón was able to buy it for his land reform program."

He looked up from the ruins to the trees encircling the clearing. "Only the trees remain. Don Pedro sent for trees from all over Argentina for this monte. They came from the mountains of

ground. Sometime in 1942 she disappeared and was presumed dead by German hands.

Diana blew out the candle on the table next to their bed and snuggled gratefully into his arms. "How did the house in the monte burn down? Do you know?" she whispered.

"No. No one really knows. Dragonetti said it was probably a kerosene lamp that had been left burning. But the odd thing is that it happened on Christmas Eve, the day don Pedro's daughter died, when everyone was away in Las Rosas attending the funeral."

name is Maria. I'm Rosa's sister-in-law. And those are my children," she said, pointing to two little boys sitting on the bare brown earth in front of the small cottage, staring at Philip.

An old, heavy-set woman was sweeping this hard-packed earth with a primitively crafted straw broom. "And this is my mother!" explained Rosa. The old woman's eyes registered surprise, almost shock, as she peered keenly into Diana's. Her feet were bare and broad and her legs thick with varicose veins. She said nothing. She did not reach for Diana's outstretched hand but held onto her broom as though grafted to it.

A hand-operated water pump stood outside the open front door, and chickens, ducks, and a few geese scurried about the yard. One of the geese came toward Philip, frightening him. As he retreated, he fell back over an old tricycle and started to cry. The two little boys did not move or express any emotion at all. But their mother Maria ran to Philip and kneeled down, pressing him against her meager bosom, trying to comfort him.

"*Pobrecito! Pobrecito!* Poor little one!" she crooned.

He escaped from her embrace and held on tightly to Diana's legs while she explained why she had come, holding out a shiny four-liter aluminum milk can with a fine wooden handle. "I've come to buy some milk, for the little one," she patted Philip's head. "Señor Montoya told me you would have some to sell."

Rosa nodded. "Of course! Come inside." Maria and Alberto followed. But the old woman still stood, clutching her broom, staring after Diana.

There was little furniture inside the front room and what there was appeared to have been made on the farm. The underside of the roughly tiled cottage roof served as the ceiling. The floor was laid with uneven, handmade bricks that had recently been washed; small pools of water lay in depressions in the floor. But in front of one of the two windows stood a highly polished, pedal-operated sewing machine, inlaid with mother-of-pearl.

Maria introduced Diana to her husband, who did not at all resemble his brother. He was sitting at a dining table at the other end of the long, narrow room, listening to a transistor radio. Unlike his younger brother Alberto, who had greeted her eagerly, the older Berrato son barely acknowledged the introduction. He simply looked up and peered at her through glasses so thick Diana could not see his eyes and wondered if he could see hers. He nodded and returned to his radio.

"Of course," Rosa agreed.

After that, there seemed to be nothing more to say. The women stared silently at her, especially old Mrs. Berrato, as though she and Philip had come from another planet. The Berrato children continued to stare at Philip from the open doorway. When Diana urged him to go out and play with them, he replied by clutching even more tightly to her hand. The only sound in the room was that of a plaintive tango coming from the radio, punctuated now and then by the cackling of a hen outside in the yard.

Mrs. Berrato broke the suspense by rising and returning from the kitchen with a tray of tiny liquor glasses filled with orange liquor. "Our own," she said proudly.

"Oh, no thank you!" Diana replied, getting up to leave. "I didn't mean to bother you like this so early in the morning." And she moved toward the door, thanking them again for the milk.

On her way out, she looked closely at the sewing machine. "How beautiful," she commented with genuine admiration.

The old woman explained, "That was my wedding present when I was a girl in Italy. *Piamonte*, you know," she added loftily. "It's almost sixty years old, but it still works like new. I've made everything on this farm with that machine," she murmured, almost to herself, caressing it lovingly, one gnarled finger tracing over the word *Singer* engraved upon it in elaborate gold script. "Everything. Coveralls, dresses, the boy's suits...*everything*. It was the only thing we had when we came to *this* country," she concluded, looking out the door, pointing to the land, as though accusing it of some kind of treachery.

Once outside in the sunshine, everyone appeared more relaxed, almost relieved. The old Mrs. Berrato shook hands with Diana, saying, "It's too bad you missed Mr. Berrato, my husband. He's retired now, you know. It's my sons and Rosa who work the land. Maria and I keep the house and the vegetable garden. It's Mr. Berrato who goes into Las Rosas now every morning to get the bread and meat. He should be returning any moment."

Then the other family members shook Diana's hand, except for the older brother who remained inside with his radio. Her hand felt like a useless piece of putty in their rough, powerful grasps. The last to shake hands was Maria, the young, shy mother. They, too, were rough hands, cracked and red, the knuckles bulging—as coarse a pair of hands as those Diana had seen on the cod fishermen she had known as a child during summers spent on the coast of Maine.

As Diana climbed into the pickup, the old woman pressed her arm and whispered, *"Be careful of storms.* I shall soon bring you something that can help you."

Puzzled, Diana looked down into her upturned face for an explanation, but the woman only grinned weakly back at her. So she thanked her as though she knew what she meant. When she started the engine and began to drive off everyone waved, and the shy Maria called out boldly, *"Hasta la próxima, si Dios quiere!"*

The dogs leapt up from their posts, and, barking and snarling, chased the pickup all the way to the gate.

Once back on the colony road, Diana passed a Model T Ford. The driver looked at her curiously, almost angrily. He was an old man with a small, infinitely wrinkled face. From her rear-view mirror Diana saw the Model T turn into the Berrato farm and crawl slowly toward the tiny monte which surrounded the primitive cottage from which she had just come.

When she told Michael of her visit, of the poverty she had witnessed, she blurted out, "What do you think? Do you really think we can make it? They have double the land we have, and they've been working it for twenty years—"

"They don't know how to farm. That's all," he replied, without any hesitation.

"But three or four cents for a quart of milk? At this rate how can we ever repay the loan for the milking equipment? And their hands, Michael, you should see the hands of the women!"

"Why are you worried about your hands? I'm surprised at you. Aren't rough hands a small enough price for you to pay for this kind of life? Our being together? Working together? They will be like a badge for you to wear proudly."

"Of course," she acknowledged, ashamed of her vanity, as he took her delicate hands in his, their soft white skin as transparent as fine china. He pressed them to his lips, telling her, "This afternoon, while Philip is napping, I'm going to take you into the monte."

At one P.M. they left Alex outside Philip's door, and, carrying a blanket in one hand, Michael led Diana by the other to the monte. Instead of returning to the ruins, she showed him the orchard she had discovered, and he selected a shady sheltered spot under an orange tree in full bloom, not far from the protection of the laurel hedge. There, he spread out the blanket.

As she sat down staring up at the sapphire sky she asked, laugh-

"It is *love!*" he answered as he covered her body with the fragrant white blossoms, and looking into her dark eyes called her "the eternal woman." He caressed her everywhere, joy on his face, hunger in his fingertips. "You are the earth, the sea, the sky, everything for me, and I want to live in you forever."

Then he buried his face once more in the thick soft curls between her thighs, which were sweet now with the perfume of the orange blossoms that clung to them. He reached up and grasped one of his two doves, rubbing its beak hard, without mercy now, between his two fingers. When she was ready, when she could stand it no longer, she begged him to enter her.

Michael made love in French, the language of his youth, murmuring adoring phrases that came to her from above like the chorus at the beginning of the end of a great symphony. Until it happened. The little death for him, the surging ecstasy for her, like a fully arisen sea crashing against the land, wave after wave.

Somewhere a dog was barking in the sea. Barking and barking as the waters calmed and rolled away from the land. Diana sat up, pushing Michael away, telling him, "Something is wrong. Alex is calling us."

They threw on their clothes as quickly as they could. Leaving the blanket behind, they pushed their way through the laurel hedge that tore at Diana's hair, scratched her arms. Running back down the shadowy road, they scrambled over the gate, not bothering to open it. On the other side they could see a car parked near the casco, and Alex was barking furiously at its occupants.

"Of all times to have visitors," Diana hissed.

"Damn!" Michael agreed.

"Eggs! Oh, thank you."

"My husband told me you have no *chickens*!" she exclaimed, as though Diana might as well be without water, or even air.

"No. Not as yet."

"But, doña Diana, what a shame!"

The fact that this woman knew her first name, as had the Berratos, also surprised her. But then they were neighbors....

Montoya's father was a great hulk of a man who had some difficulty extricating himself from behind the wheel of the car. He was an old man, but, as he lumbered up to Michael, swinging and swaying under the burden of his great weight, his eyes were as sharp as his son's, and his handshake strong as he addressed Michael as don Miguel.

Diana invited the family into the house, but the men preferred to stay outside and inspect the machinery. Once inside the kitchen, Señor Montoya's wife looked it over quickly but made no comment. She had obviously been briefed by her husband on the strange things it contained.

While Diana prepared coffee, the older Señora Montoya and her daughter, who appeared either nervous or simply peevish, peeked timidly into the rest of the rooms. Montoya's wife apparently didn't want to leave the kitchen and continued to speak about chickens. "Can I send you over a few?" she offered. "To get started?"

"Well...I would prefer to wait until I can build a hen house."

"Nonsense!" the woman laughed. "Chickens don't need houses. They like to run *free*. They're happier like that and lay better, you can bet!" She winked at Diana. "You know what I mean."

"But won't they run away?"

"Oh, no. They know where they belong. They *like* to stay near the house. Just give them water and a little grain now and then. They prefer to find the rest for themselves in the fields."

"But how do you know where to collect the eggs?"

The woman looked at her, puzzled, as though wondering if Diana was stupid or if she was trying to trick her.

"Well...you know. You will just know. They find themselves a sheltered spot." She spoke slowly, as though to a child. "You just have to watch. And *listen*. Of course," she relented, "if you *want* to build a hen house. I've heard that some people do that. If you've got the wood and money to spare...there would be no *harm* in it." She hesitated. "But it would just be a waste," she concluded.

As she spoke, Diana heard her mother-in-law tell her daughter,

"Yes. The daughter of don Pedro. The last of the Casildas. Mrs. Berrato worked for her when she was young. Kept house for her. In there. In that house that burned down. Oh, she has told me what a wonderful thing it was to see. Like a museum. Don Pedro imported beautiful things from all over the world for that house." She turned back to Diana, and in a low voice added, "As have you."

"And there is nothing left."

"No."

"Do you know how it burned down?"

The woman stared at Diana with her strange, misty eyes without answering, until her daughter-in-law called to Diana from the edge of the orchard. As she turned from the older woman to reply, Diana had the curious notion that the woman thought she should know why the house had burned down and that her question was some kind of a trick.

Instead of replying, Señora Montoya glanced over at her daughter-in-law standing with her hands on her ample hips, her legs spread apart. The lady from Spain explained, "She is *Italian*." But she smiled as she said this, just enough to let Diana know she had long since stopped caring about this regrettable fact.

When the Montoyas left, Michael followed Diana into the kitchen and slammed the door after him. He was angry.

"I think it was a nice visit," she assured him. "I think they liked us."

"You always assume too much. They were curious. That's all. I think the old man would have liked to have had this campo himself. He was the administrator of this colony for the past twenty years and would never let this parcel be sold. He was saving it until the last. For his retirement, which he did last year when the colony was dissolved after all the farmers had finished paying for their land. His son has rented the land on this campo many times, and I suspect he's furious now that he never bothered to apply for it. I know that Dragonetti doesn't like him. He warned me about him."

"About what?"

"Nothing, really. Just that he's a troublemaker. And not well liked around here, either. But I can understand that. He's been collecting the payments from all these Italian farmers for years. And, being of Spanish origin, considers himself superior to them."

"The old man's daughter-in-law was nice. So funny! She's determined I should have chickens. And I liked his wife."

HE large, open circular well outside the former dormitory cookhouse was dry. Lined with bricks, it was thirty feet deep and filled with debris. "There has to be another source nearby," Michael said, surveying the area. "That old well has been dry for many, many years and a new well must have been drilled. And not far from the casco."

Within an hour he found it, covered up by a few outsized old bricks hidden under a clump of pampa grass near the window of Philip's bedroom and forty feet from the old well. He was jubilant. "Here it is!" He hooked up the powerful new pump he had brought back from Buenos Aires to the Lister generator he had installed in the cookhouse and began pumping.

The water came out in a trickle at first and then gushed upward into the air like a miniature geyser. It was foul. Full of sulfur, it was thoroughly undrinkable.

"Wait and see," Michael advised and kept on pumping, filling the air with the odor of rotten eggs.

"Why the sulfur?" Diana cried, her heart sinking lower and lower as the generator boomed on hour after hour without producing anything but dark, evil-smelling water.

"Because the pampas were once an inland sea. But there are pockets of fresh water, I know. Estancia La Argentina would not have chosen this site for their homestead, out of all the other areas they could have chosen, without having found one of these pockets."

By nightfall he had still no success. Nothing but dirty water. "We will keep on pumping," he told Diana, "all through the night." And he filled the generator's fuel tank with diesel before climbing into bed next to Diana. "Have faith," he told her. "There *has* to be fresh water here. I know it."

He didn't sleep, though, and got up several times to check the water. Diana couldn't sleep, either, her heart beating along to the thump, thump, thump of the noisy generator. "Anything yet?" she asked the last time he returned before the sun rose.

Tired, covered with oil and stinking clothes, he yelled at her. "No! But will you leave me alone? Don't you trust me?"

Angry and scared, she turned over and tried to sleep, all the

Michael came around the casco, and when she told him what had happened and showed him the candle, he laughed.

"That's one I've never heard before. It must be an Italian superstition. From Piamonte."

"What kind of storms, I wonder?"

"The pamperos."

"You think so? A strange idea. I have the feeling she meant something else. You know, she once worked here in the big house."

"Yes?"

"Montoya's mother told me she worked for the Casildas when she was young. I wish I could get to know her better."

"I wouldn't ask too many questions, if I were you."

"Why not? Why shouldn't we know about the people who used to own this land?"

"The Consejo. That's who used to own this land."

"All right." She was surprised by his reaction. Perhaps he was only trying to be cautious. "But I wish that Philip could be friends, though, with the children. They are the closest boys of his age around here, and he needs friends. He would learn to speak—"

"Those kind of people would never feel comfortable with us."

"I know. Still, it was kind of her to give me this."

When Michael decided it was time to hire a peón, they went to the headquarters of the Farm Laborers' Union in Las Rosas to find one. The office was a dark and squalid place, full of men of all ages in rumpled clothes, many of which had obviously been slept in. All had sweat scarves tied around their necks; some wore ordinary slacks and shirts, and some were dressed like derelict gauchos, with soiled *bombachas* and crushed and broken sombreros.

"*¡El Inglés!*" The Englishman! Diana heard whispers among the men as they crossed the threshold.

Since there were no chairs, most of the men were sitting on the floor, propped up against the wall, smoking hand-rolled cigarettes of coarse black tobacco. Two containers of *maté*, in the shape of a gourd, were being passed from one set of dark lips to the other as each man took his sip of this bitter, strong tea from a silver straw they called a *bombilla*.

The harassed-looking little man at the desk appeared very upset at the sight of them and looked pleadingly around the room. But everyone remained silent, and no one came forward. Beads of anxious perspiration broke out on his swarthy face before his eyes fo-

fair fight," he assured her, "but that time, in the game of knives my father had been so good at, death won."

He, along with many young men of his age, preferred to find work in the town, where he lived with his mother, taking care of her. But on the other hand, Diana learned, he and his friends did not work in the city like many others of his kind who crowded the outskirts of places like Buenos Aires, Rosario, Córdoba, or Santa Fe, huddled together in shanty towns. No, the young men of the village could not alienate themselves *that* far from their roots, which were in the soil of the pampas. From the village, they could always escape back to the land somewhere when they felt a need to do so. "Whereas in the city," Rafael explained, "Everyone knows it is evil. *There*, one can get trapped. *One might not even have enough to eat.*"

But now that the country was experiencing a recession, thousands were out of work. There certainly was no work in Las Rosas for him at the moment, and that was why he had agreed to help Michael out. "Just to keep my hand in, so to speak," he shrugged. "Besides," he added, "I hear he intends to build things, and I like that kind of work."

The first thing they built was their Australian tank, to store the water pumped from their well. Michael bought all the material—the sand, stone, chalk, cement, iron, and brick—in Las Rosas, and Diana transported it in the pickup, making several trips a day. Rafael and Michael took turns mixing batches of the concrete and pouring it over the foundation of precisely woven iron rods. Rafael worked by Michael's side all day long uttering hardly a word. He appeared happy, whistling a little tune now and then and taking pride in his work. He never jumped from one step of the project to another until absolutely sure that he had completed the previous one satisfactorily.

Once, when Diana complimented him on his workmanship, Rafael told her, "Oh, I've laid some bricks before. Mixed some concrete. A child of the pampas knows how to do a little bit of everything." A rare smile broadened his mustached lips, and his dark young eyes brightened with pride.

He later explained that he had watched very carefully the men who had come in to pave the main road of Las Rosas, hoping that when it came time to pave the roads around the central plaza, he would be able to get a job with them.

Rafael never wanted to enter the casco. From the very first day,

precisely at the moment dawn exploded into day behind him, they saw, instead, a lone horseman. It wasn't until he was well up their road, trotting at a leisurely pace, that they realized the gaucho was Rafael, and as he rode toward the casco, crossing the field where the ombú stood, Diana could tell by his smile that the horse was for them.

From the moment he mounted the mare, Michael was at ease, riding her as though he had been raised in her saddle. Even Diana, who had rarely ridden before, felt comfortable on Mora. An old pro, the mare was twenty-one years old and had been herding cows for eighteen. Before that, in her filly days, she had chased polo balls. The color of woven flax, Mora had the grace, delicate legs, and fine head of a polo horse, but her strong, thick body was that of a working farm horse.

She also had her idiosyncrasies and could fake a limp when she didn't feel like working, but she would always know where the cows were, Rafael assured them, even in the darkest of nights. They would be her business, and she would keep an eye on them. She understood them, as well as their calves, and knew all their tricks.

As Michael and Rafael built the Australian tank, Diana carefully replaced the casco's window panes with glass Michael showed her how to cut to size. It was difficult at first, but by the time she had finished putting seventy-eight panes in place, she was an expert at the job.

The tank was completed by the end of summer, and then Rafael began making the concrete blocks for the dairy with the hand press they had brought with them from England. Diana made daily trips into Las Rosas, hauling back the necessary sand, pebbles, and concrete while Michael wired the casco for electricity and installed the plumbing. As she had planned, Diana and he turned the little dark room with the meat hooks in the rafters into a modern bathroom, complete with tub and sink, shower, toilet, even bidet, and shiny white tiles on the walls.

Although she worked for weeks in this room, Diana never completely lost the feeling she had experienced on the first day she had stepped into it: that there was a presence of some kind inside this room. As she worked, she felt she was somehow physically pushing this presence aside in order to accomplish her task. And every time she crossed the threshold to take up her job anew, she would feel it again. It did not go away; yet it didn't frighten her and she became accustomed to it.

One day after lunch, when Michael and Rafael had taken off to the neighboring village of Las Parejas in search of more building supplies, Diana put Philip down for his nap, washed the dishes, and went into the new bathroom to wash her face before taking her own siesta. The generator had been cut, and the ensuing silence was soft and sweet.

As she passed the cool wet cloth over her face, she looked up and saw another face in the mirror above the sink. Whirling around, she found no one standing in the doorway behind her. She ran out into the bedroom. No one. Quickly opening the door, she stepped out onto the gallery, but again there was no one, and she could see no sign of dust in the air from someone having passed on the road.

Alex, stretched out flat on the cool brick floor of the gallery, merely lifted his head to her briefly, as though to say, "What's the matter with you?" Then lowered it again and blinked his eyes, his tail moving lazily back and forth.

The face had been that of a man, she was sure. Neither smiling nor menacing. It was almost emotionless, composed as is a portrait painted on a black canvas from a bygone era. She was fully awake and alert, not even tired. She was certain she had not been hallucinating. Yet, she must have been, she decided as she lay down, all of her senses trembling with astonishment.

It could not have been a ghost, she reasoned. Ghosts don't manifest themselves in broad daylight in the face of a shining new medicine cabinet mirror, framed with chrome. If it had to be through a mirror, why not the old mirror, blotched with age, that was in the bedroom, and of whose origins she knew nothing? She closed her eyes, determined to forget what had happened. She was not going to let the Montoyas or Berratos frighten her with their ridiculous superstitions.

She said nothing about the face in the mirror to Michael when he returned. After a few days, her memory of the incident faded, as though it had been a dream.

But a month later, when everyone was home, and in the same place, and at approximately the same time of day—during the hour of the siesta when everyone but Diana was sleeping, when all motors had been cut and silence reigned over the land, when even the songbirds in the orchard had gone away to sleep in their nests in the monte and the wind itself had lain down to rest—she saw the face again.

I N late summer Michael turned over the twenty acres of wild grasses in front of the casco with the rotavator. This powerful machine cut into the virgin soil as though it were butter and ground up the earth into fine particles all in one operation, eliminating the need for disking or raking. He planted a variety of pasture seeds, including alfalfa and white clover, imported from the United States, scientifically selected for high milk production the year 'round.

"It's expensive," he admitted to Diana, "but it's guaranteed for five years."

Rafael continued making cement blocks for the dairy and with the arrival of autumn, he and Michael had finished the walls of the milk house, one tandem stall, a long narrow paved and securely fenced holding entry area for cows waiting to be milked, and an exit ramp. Michael hoped to have the entire dairy completed by the end of the winter with four tandem stalls, two on either side of the central operating work station. This would permit one person to milk seventy-five top-producing dairy cows in less than one-and-a-half hours.

The post office was always Diana's first stop every time she went to Las Rosas. Though she rarely received any personal mail from abroad, she could not help but experience a vague sense of hope each time she opened her box that she would. When a letter did arrive for her, with the magical red, white, and blue symbols signifying a letter from overseas—even if it was only from the U.S. Department of Agriculture—she would immediately rip open the envelope and read it.

Her mother wrote infrequently. Diana knew she had not approved of her leaving the stage and her sudden marriage to Michael, though she never said so. She had never visited Diana in England, and when Philip was born, all Diana received was a note telling her she could be assured that Philip's birth defect didn't run in her family. Diana's younger sister and brother, busy with their own families, only sent cards at Christmas.

One morning she turned from her box to find herself looking directly into the pale blue eyes of a stocky, ruddy-faced man of

strategically here and there. A band was playing tangos beneath a great spreading Black Forest oak set in the center of a circular brick terrace in front of the main house. It was not a typical, fortress-like estancia house. Rather, it resembled a Bavarian chalet.

The visitors were well-dressed business men from Buenos Aires, Rosario, Santa Fe, and Córdoba who mingled with prosperous ranchers from all over Argentina, along with a few genuine gauchos—the last of that dying breed of men who once rode over the land unchallenged by either fences or the law. They appeared to carry their fortunes on their backs, as they always had. Their accordion boots were made from leather of an extraordinary quality: strong, yet as supple as kid gloves. Most of the gauchos wore bombachas of impeccably white linen, with their thousand pleats razor sharp. These singular pants were secured with belts lined with valuable coins, joined together by elaborately worked buckles of silver and gold, studded with jewels. A sheathed dagger richly worked and encrusted with semi-precious stones was thrust into the back of each gaucho's belt. Their loose-fitting, long-sleeved shirts were of the finest cotton, and around their necks they wore silk scarves in a variety of brilliant colors. All sported thick, bushy, turned-down mustaches like the one on the face Diana had seen in the mirror.

Children played about in the afternoon sunshine, and Philip overcame his shyness enough to leave Diana's side to watch them swing on the swings that had been set up for them. There were also ponies for them to ride, all under the watchful eyes of a few ferocious-looking gauchos who had been commissioned to take charge of these activities.

The guests were drinking champagne served to them by white-gloved waiters. The scene was one of extraordinary affluence, and Diana was thankful she and Michael had dressed for the occasion. She had chosen her favorite frock of emerald green voile that went so well with her honey-colored hair. It clung elegantly to her tall, slim dancer's body, and billowed out softly around her as she moved about, like the wings of a tropical butterfly. Michael wore his well-cut navy blue blazer, gray flannel slacks, formal white shirt with gold cuff links, and his favorite dark blue-and-red striped silk tie.

Carlos Bauer had been waiting for them. He and Michael cordially shook hands. "Welcome," he told him, studying him appraisingly, admiring what he saw. "So happy you could come," he told Diana, looking directly into her eyes. "Let me introduce you both to some people I think you should meet."

And as he took her hand, he added, somewhat ruefully, "After all, it could be said we're exiles, too. Just like these people."

"Michael!" She withdrew her hand. "It's not the same. How can you say that?"

At that moment Carlos Bauer was by their side, "Come. Let me introduce you to the Admiral. His name is Ricardo Hoffman, but everyone calls him the Admiral. He was an Admiral in the German Navy during World War I, and he manages Santa Clara, the largest estancia in the province, which is twice as big as the Southern Cross. It begins just up the road from you and extends all the way to Iturraspe. He's someone you should know."

Although thin and frail, the Admiral had merry blue eyes, full of life and intelligence. Diana couldn't help but like him as he graciously took her hand and pressed it to his lips. And Michael greeted his vivacious wife, who was called simply *La Violeta*, in a similar manner.

"She was once the belle of Montevideo," Carlos explained as the distinguished couple moved off, and, noting Michael's look of undisguised admiration as it followed *La Violeta*, he added, laughing, "Yes. She's broken many a heart in her time. And she's still breaking hearts, I understand. The Admiral is her third husband. But now, I would like you to meet my wife."

Marlena Bauer was standing quite alone under the spreading oak, looking out over her guests. Michael shook her hand, and Carlos then led him off elsewhere to introduce him to a group of English ranchers, leaving Diana alone with her. She was a large woman, a little taller than Diana, strongly built and perhaps fifteen years older. Her broad face was a mask, giving no hint of any emotions that might be hiding beneath her fixed smile. She wore her straight dark brown hair cut short, like a man's, and dressed conservatively in a tweed skirt with a tailored white blouse and square-laced walking shoes. The only hint of joy in her appearance was a red rose in her lapel, and her skin shone with the freshness of a young girl.

She spoke in flawless English, yet hesitantly, as though from a distance. Outside of Buenos Aires, Marlena Bauer was the first woman Diana had met on the pampas who could speak her language. She observed Diana with appraising eyes for fully a minute. When she finally smiled, she told her, "I hope you will like me. I know I can help you, and I hope you will let me. Carlos would like that."

the war, after the fall of Berlin, he and his wife managed to escape to Argentina. Through *Switzerland*," she added, as though it mattered. "He doesn't live here regularly, though. Campo life doesn't agree with him, and he lives most of the year in Villa Gesell or Buenos Aires. Carlos manages the Tres Marias for him."

When Marlena invited her into the house, she found the three Marias seated around a long table covered with heavy white linen and piled high with German delicacies and pastries of all kinds. In contrast to the bright sunshine on the lawn, the house was dark and cool. As Diana's eyes adjusted to the subdued light in the large dining hall, the three old women appeared tiny, gnome-like, and severe. They were dressed identically in long gray skirts and wore gray blouses with high lace collars. They had their thin gray hair tightly drawn back in tiny buns, and they seemed like living relics of the steel-willed German women who had pioneered the Midwestern plains of the United States a generation before. They did not speak English and looked right through Diana, barely acknowledging Marlena's introductions, turning away from her to greet a group of German friends who followed Diana into the room.

Ernesto, Carlos' cousin, on the other hand, was a huge man with a generous smile for her. His light brown hair was thinning, exposing an unusually large dome, but he still had the appearance of a man in the prime of life. He exhibited that special kind of self-assurance peculiar to men of property who are used to having their affairs run by competent employees. The sort of man one felt free, even obliged, to confide in.

His wife, Agatha, was a pretty, middle-aged woman, who smiled sweetly and earnestly at the guests. She was slim, with fine, delicate features and pale eyes, and her short blonde hair waved softly about her head. She wore an elegantly cut bright blue linen dress which complemented her fair, flawless complexion, and she reminded Diana of a prima ballerina she had once known, as she moved gracefully, almost on her toes, from one guest to another. Taking both of Diana's hands in hers, she said in perfect English, and with great warmth, "How nice for Marlena that you have come to live here. She is so alone and needs a friend. Do you have children?"

"Yes." Diana looked over to where Philip stood quietly watching the other children play.

"Good. Bring him to me. Let me meet him. Marlena does not, you know. He will be good for her, too."

When it came time to eat, Carlos thoughtfully placed Diana,

She's in Texas now. Goes there every year for the cattle fairs." He lowered his voice. "But she wouldn't be here, anyway. She was a heroine in the Dutch Underground during the War. Hates Germans, of course. But doesn't hesitate to exploit them. Or anybody, as a matter of fact. Just wait. You'll find out when she returns and hears about you."

"Is she really a Duchess?" Diana asked.

"Sure is."

Another Anglo-Argentine, Ricardo Andrews, sitting across from them asked Michael, "When are you going to start up that modern dairy we've been hearing so much about?" A sportsman raised on the pampas, he was well known, Denitz told Michael and Diana, for his skill in polo. He had also recently acquired a small plane and was learning how to fly. He was younger than the others, in his mid-twenties, thin, wiry, blond with wide-open eager brown eyes that appeared to stare at the world with astonishment, as though he had just been born into it and was amazed at what he saw. He was accompanied by his fiancée, a young socialite from Buenos Aires who was delighting in the company of these cattle men.

"Just as soon as I get the dairy finished," Michael grinned confidently. "Should be around the end of winter."

"Why wait so long? I've got ten fine cows I could sell you now. They're ready to drop their calves any minute. Purebreds, too! And you won't have to pay before a year's time. It will be worth it to me to see if your pipeline system works. Here, we're still milking by hand with the calf tied to the mother's leg. The dairymen won't believe it can be done otherwise."

Michael hesitated. "But I don't have a corral. No interior fences—"

"You have a horse, don't you?"

"I haven't even gotten a roof on the dairy yet. And only one stall operational."

"That's all you need. You don't need a roof. And I don't know when I'll have another lot I'd be willing to let go like this. After all, it's *only* ten cows I'm talking about," he laughed, as his companions grinned, leaning forward, all eyes on Michael, waiting for his reply.

"Oh, please do!" Andrews' fiancée urged, smiling broadly at Diana. "I'll come and visit you after we are married!"

"Of course," Diana replied.

"When will you come to pick them up?" Andrews asked.

was English. They had first gone to your country. To California. The wife's baby was murdered by your Indians there. So they took a boat and traveled all the way down the west coast of South America, around the Horn, and up the east coast until they found their way here. Extraordinary.... Why do *you* want to come here now?"

"Michael has always wanted to farm," she replied simply.

"Why not in the United States? That is *your* country, no?"

"Oh...." Diana felt as though she were being grilled, and by a professional at that. Ernesto was no longer making polite conversation. "He just likes Argentina better," she smiled sweetly.

"You dance beautifully. Have you ever been on the stage?"

Diana laughed.

"If not, you should have been."

"Thank you."

"Well," he decided, "you and your husband should do well. We're all exiles here. You will feel comfortable with us."

Holding her loosely as they waltzed around the terrace, he told her, "All of us...running from something, all feeding on our hopeless dreams of what was and what could have been.... Welcome to the club."

Diana wanted to protest. She was not a member of *his* club. Nor was she an exile. She averted her face from his until the dance came to an end, realizing that Ernesto Bauer, despite his affable manner and his wealth, was a very unhappy man.

When they were ready to take their leave, Carlos again congratulated Michael on his purchase of Andrews' cows, assuring him they were of good stock. Michael took this opportunity to ask Carlos the question he had come to ask: the possibility of buying semen from the Southern Cross.

Carlos answered, "Buy? No. I'll *give* it to you. It would be good publicity for us. If you are successful, why, who knows? The Southern Cross might be able to start a business locally among the small farmers like you. It could even spread out to other parts of the country. *Dios!* You and I might even find ourselves in business together. Yes!" He clasped Michael's hand firmly. "We will work together," he assured him.

Diana said good-bye to Marlena, daring to kiss her cheek, feeling the woman blush under this impulsive gesture of friendship, Argentine style.

~ Part II ~
Learning the Land

Here windy words are nothing worth,
Nor doctors of high degree;
Here many that think they know a lot,
Would find their wits tied up in a knot;
For this is a door with a different lock,
And the gaucho has the key.

Martín Fierro, by José Hernández

~

E shall use the electric fencing to make our corral."
Together with Diana and Rafael, Michael unpacked the box
from England containing the metal stakes, the insulators, the thick
wire, and finally the control box. When Michael showed them how
it worked, Rafael was intrigued, and amused.

He took off his crushed black felt hat and scratched his head,
smiling. "I don't know, Patrón. I don't think a single wire, electrified or not, is going to hold one of our cows."

"Well, we'll see. Now I'm off!" And he climbed into the pickup
heading in the direction of El Trebol where Andrews' estancia, La
Porteña, was located.

Diana and Rafael worked all day setting up the fencing around
the dairy. Rafael hung around as long as he dared before nightfall,
but still the cows had not arrived. Finally, when it was almost dark,
he prepared to take off for Las Rosas on his bicycle in the twilight.
"I'll be back, Señora, with the first light," he promised.

"Oh, God, Rafael, can't you stay just for one night?"

"No. My mother would worry. Anyway," he scanned the dark-
ening horizon, "I doubt if they'll show up tonight."

But they did. At ten P.M. the cattle truck drove up, but without
Michael. "He had a breakdown on the road," the driver explained,
looking down at Diana from the cab of his truck, the motor still
running. "He'll be along later. Where's your corral?" he asked,
looking around and seeing nothing in the headlights of his truck
but the half-finished dairy, still without a roof over the single stall.

"Can't we wait until my husband returns?"

"*Por favor, Señora.* No. I must be in Rosario by morning. Just
show me the way to your corral."

When he saw what it was, he exclaimed, *"This?"*

"Yes. It's electrified."

"*Dios*! Señora, you must understand these are half-wild animals
I have in this truck. They are not like your European cows, raised
in barns. Why, the pasture I just took them from is larger than this
whole campo, and before me they've never even *seen* a man, except
to be vaccinated."

"It's all right," Diana insisted.

Diana, too, was excited. "But where are the calves?"

"They get left in the pasture. Don't worry, the mothers will return to find them and feed them. Right now, all they want is water. But first they must be milked. Somehow we must get those three into the stall and milk them, or their udders will become infected and ruined."

Mora had been saddled, waiting for Michael, who quickly galloped off to herd the cows into the makeshift corral.

He told Diana, "You stand next to the entrance to the corral and be prepared to divert them into it as I herd them from behind."

But as soon as the cows saw a horseman, they panicked and came thundering down the road towards her, with Michael after them.

She suddenly found herself facing an express train, coming at full speed. Terrified, she stepped aside to let the cows roar by. Michael galloped on after them, yelling at her, "Why did you do that?"

"Because I'm afraid of cows!" she cried after him, shaking like a hunted deer.

"This is a hell of a time to find that out!" he shouted back.

She wondered, desperate, why Rafael hadn't come.

The second time the cows approached, she was again unable to stand her ground and stepped aside at the last moment as the cows thundered by.

Michael swore at her, galloping past after them, "Damn you! You bitch!"

Stunned, Diana's terror turned to rage. As the cows came galloping toward her for the third time, she screamed at them. Darting forward as they came closer, she waved her arms frantically.

The animals turned from this woman gone mad and found themselves trapped in the makeshift corral.

Milking them was something else. Michael could not separate the ones who had to be milked from those that didn't. So he ran them all through the single stall several times with both the entrance and exit doors open, hoping to acquaint them with it and calm their fears. The cows were so frightened they didn't even notice that they had to walk up steps in order to enter and pass through. But when Michael closed the exit gate, they refused to enter the stall, seeing that they had no way to escape.

"We'll have to trick them," he said. "You hide around the corner of the building. Just as the cow we have to milk is about to exit,

Michael managed to untie the rope around her hind legs. He prodded her, poked and beat her, trying to force her up. But she would not move. She took his blows without flinching, as though she were already dead. Diana watched Michael with horror as fury contorted his face. His entire body shook with uncontrollable rage.

"*Please! Let her alone!*" she sobbed. This was a part of him she had never seen. Never suspected existed.

"No!" he shouted. "If you can't stand it, go back to the house! And take that damned dog with you!"

"*Please!*" she begged, feeling as though she was about to be sick.

"You don't understand! If I can't tame my first cow, I might as well pack up and go back to England!"

Perspiration soaked him, almost blinded him as he continued punishing the animal until she eventually gave in and struggled up from the concrete floor. He quickly reached for the machine lying in the dung where it had fallen between her legs. He was not quick enough, however, and she kicked his hand viciously before he was able to pull back.

Milk now poured from the cow's udder. Once the machine had sucked at her, once the letdown process had started, she was unable to stop it, and this sent her into a renewed state of rage. Again, she reared up on her hind legs and hung herself up over the front gate. This time it was Diana who faced her, screaming and sobbing and beating her back with a piece of fence post that finally broke over the cow's head. The blow sent the cow crashing back down onto the floor of the stall, now slippery with a mixture of milk, dung, and urine.

The cow struggled to her feet almost immediately, aware now of the blows she would receive from Michael if she stayed on the floor. She still would not surrender, though, and kicked against the bars with renewed vigor. There seemed to be no limit to her strength.

Michael waited, tense as a panther ready to spring upon its prey. When the cow paused, he sprang forward and slipped the rope around her legs. He attached the machine to her teats before she could regain her breath.

This time, as the milk flowed from her, she didn't resist as much as before. The painful pressure in her udder was being relieved. Once relieved, however, she remembered where she was. After a few minutes of being milked, she again protested violently against her tormentor, clawing at the machine with her harnessed hooves.

up steps, they wouldn't believe me."

"Really? Why not?"

"Señora," Rafael put down his shovel and looked at her carefully. "No Argentine cow walks up steps and lets herself be milked without her calf. They say it must be the language you use when you talk to them."

"But it's only English we speak." And I sing, she might have added, because she had started serenading them as well.

Leaning on his shovel, Rafael pushed back his crumpled black felt hat and mused, "Perhaps the cows understand it.... I've heard of an Italian farmer who can cure calves that get worms. From a distance. Just by speaking to them in his special language. They come out and go away."

"Rafael," Diana frowned, "you know how we had to beat the cows up those steps at first. It's not the language."

"I know," he smiled slowly. Pulling his hat down over his forehead once more, he turned back to the hole he was digging. "But it's true about the Italian farmer."

hoof and wrapped what he called "the calving rope" around his waist, as though he was preparing to pull someone out of the bottom of a well.

As the cow bore down and tried to push her calf out into the world, he helped her by pulling away from her with each contraction. Bit by bit, the calf appeared, its forelegs stretched and pinned to either side of its head—looking like a diver, slick with water and oil, ready to plunge into a pool. Finally assisted by a tremendous final shove from its mother, the calf rushed through the narrow opening and completed its dive, crashing down, wet and glistening, onto the ground below.

"Male? Female?" Diana asked as Michael slipped the noose off from around its ankles and cleared the mucus from its nose, breathing into its mouth to stimulate its lungs.

"Female. Now you can let her go."

Diana released the cow. Though wild, the cow did not run away. Linda's only thought was to turn to her prone calf, already beginning to shiver with cold, and lick away, with long, powerful strokes of her rough tongue, the sticky remains of the membrane-thin sac that covered it, drying its fur, rousing its body to life after its terrible struggle. Gentle, cooing sounds of welcome came from deep within her as she marveled at the life she had created.

"Where did you learn how to do this?" Diana also marveled, not only at the birth but at Michael's expertise.

"Royal Navy. We once had a stowaway on board. Pregnant she was, and the chief mate took out his book and improvised. But, of course, he didn't use a rope. Hah! Something similar, though."

As Linda sang her lullaby to her calf, the afterbirth was expelled effortlessly, and Alex, waiting outside the corral, sneaked in like a thief—almost on his belly—and dragged it away from under the cow's hooves to a grassy spot under the trees. He then proceeded to eat it.

Diana started to protest. "Let him," Michael told her. "It's very nutritious. He knows what he's doing."

This miracle of life was repeated over and over as each of the remaining six cows gave birth. The last delivery, however, was a difficult one, and it happened during the night. Diana and Michael had been keeping vigil for several hours, lying on their backs in the grass outside the corral, smoking cigarettes under an extraordinary sea of stars that sparkled like a billion bright eyes watching over

Diana, "or she'll die of pneumonia. Go to the house and bring back all the towels you can find."

While she was gone Michael and Montoya carried the cold, slippery, mucous-covered body of the rejected calf out of the corral and onto the clean grass in front of the casco. Diana dried the calf, a female, rubbing life into it as vigorously as she could until she could feel it stir beneath her strong, stroking caresses. She didn't stop for a moment until its fur was clean and fluffy, and it struggled to its feet for a brief second—before collapsing back onto the grass.

"It will never live," Montoya told her as he accepted a brandy from Michael.

"Oh, yes, she will," Diana answered him. She put her finger into its mouth, and the calf began to suck at it, struggling once again to her feet and pressing herself against Diana, trying to find milk.

"See? She *will* live."

"*A ver...a ver...to be seen....*" Montoya looked down at her, wondering. Then he turned to Michael, "But twins! *Dios me libre,*" he muttered, passing his hand over his eyes. "It's very rare. It's never happened to me, thank God."

"You know," he added, after helping himself to another drink, "for a gringo you did very well. Many of the farmers around here would have thrown up their hands and let the cow die. Or waited too long. Waited until morning and called a useless veterinarian. Is this how they do it in England? You sure must have delivered a lot of cows in your life."

Michael laughed. "I don't know. I just read a lot."

Señor Montoya looked puzzled. Then grinned. "Pulling my leg, aren't you?"

Michael laughed again. "Sure, old boy!"

While Michael drove him home, Diana made a bed for her new calf in the kitchen and stayed with it for the rest of the night. In the morning, after the milking, she carried it to the orchard where she gave it some of its mother's first milk to drink from a wine bottle capped with a spare rubber teat. The calf accepted it eagerly and even wanted to play.

Later that evening, before snuffing out the candle next to her bed, she asked Michael, "I wonder how come you know so much about birthing calves? You didn't learn everything on board that ship. And they don't teach such things in engineering schools."

"I don't know. I really don't. I guess it's just instinct."

ITH the arrival of winter, Diana learned that a house without heat on the Pampa Húmeda can be a miserable place to live. The sky is often gray all day long, the fields brown and in retreat, the air bleak and cold. Even the ombú loses its leaves and stands black and naked in the grayness of a mournful June. The winter traveled like a shadow across the land. Its only companions were the bitter southern winds and the silent but ever present drizzle that chills one's bones and makes blessed the memory of the dry, scorching days in January.

The chilling dampness of May and June could be so bad that water condensed on the inside walls of the unheated homes and ran down them in cold rivulets. The humidity also condensed on the ceilings, and sleeping under a tin roof at that time of year, Diana learned to her chagrin, could be like lying under a cold shower that has not been properly turned off.

A home without a fireplace was a poor home on the pampas, and many did not have one. Great estancias like Santa Clara and the Southern Cross had fireplaces and central heating as well. But for most farmers, the corn-cob-fired kitchen stove provided all the comfort that could be found during those dreary days when the body and mind fought the assaults of cold and dampness.

Many older people did not make it through the winter, and babies born during this time had to be strong if they were to survive. The greatest number of deaths around Las Rosas occurred just before the coming of spring. By the end of August, Diana could hear the church bells tolling every time she went to Las Rosas, encountering a funeral procession making its way through the streets. "For another poor *viejo*—old one—who didn't make it through the winter."

"Close the door!" Diana grumbled one morning in late August when Michael returned for breakfast after delivering the previous evening's and the morning's milk to the cheese factory. "It's so *cold*."

"Sorry," he smiled. "Have patience. As I've told you, once the dairy is finished I'll close in the gallery and build you a huge fireplace in the center."

Trebol and came snooping around the factory the other day. He told him about us."

"Ah...hah!"

Señor Rossio and his son drove slowly up the road to the campo the next day in a Chevrolet sedan, its newness dimmed by the winter mud of the road. A prosperous-looking businessman in his sixties, he had thick graying hair and the self-assured manners of a provincial gentleman. He extended his hand to Michael. "Don Miguel!" he exclaimed. "What a pleasure! I've heard so much about you." Turning to the young man by his side, he introduced him. "My son. Tomás."

He then bowed to Diana. She said, "Welcome. Would you like to see our dairy? It's not finished yet, but the machinery is installed."

"But, of course. From what I hear, I should be very interested."

He first admired the stalls Michael was building. "Far better designed," he admitted, his eyes narrowing, "than the clumsy wooden ones we build."

When Michael demonstrated the pipeline milking system, he told him, "Now something like that could cause a revolution in the country's dairy industry. In better times, of course, when the people will be able to afford such a machine. But with clean milk, we could export more cheese. Right now our cheese won't pass inspection by many countries. Especially the United States. Now *that* could be a big market."

Following the tour of the dairy, Señor Rossio said, "You must come and visit my factory. Meet my family. We are the largest employer in El Trebol, and," he proudly added, "despite the recession—and the subsequent fall in orders, you understand—we have not laid off a single man."

El Trebol resembled Las Rosas, but there was a smell of prosperity in El Trebol that Diana had not noticed in any of the other dusty towns in the Province of Santa Fe. Señor Rossio's factory was located in the center of town. He greeted Diana and Michael warmly, reaching in his pocket for a piece of hard candy for Philip, and gave them a tour of his factory.

In the middle of the factory yard was a little shed surrounded by grass, flowers, and a white picket fence. Inside this was a crude carpenter's bench and some tools. "That's where it all began,"

Rossio explained that only his sister Maria lived there now with a companion-maid. "Maria never married," he told them. "Oh, she could have had anyone she wanted. She was my father's favorite and could have had the biggest dowry of any girl in the town, but she preferred to remain single. She worked side by side with him, even as a little girl, and took care of him before he died. She's the real business brains of the company and keeps all the accounts. I don't know what I would do without her. No," he told them, "without Maria, I'd be lost. Absolutely *lost*."

Turning to the smaller house he said, "Now you must meet my wife. She's waiting for you."

Señora Rossio was still a beautiful woman, and in another city, another setting, she could have been taken for a dowager. She proudly gave them a tour of their home, which was crowded with overstuffed furniture, some of it protected with plastic covers. In the salon she pointed with pride at several garish mementos they had collected on a recent trip to visit family in Italy.

"Come," she said. "It is time for luncheon." They adjourned to the dining room, where the Rossio's son Tomás and daughter Lila were already seated at the table. Señora Rossio gushed over Philip, who smiled shyly back at her. She prepared a chair with a cushion on it for him, placing him next to her at the dining table, exclaiming, "All I'm waiting for are grandchildren!"

Lila, who was introduced as the assistant principal of the local high school, laughed. "I've only been married three months. We're trying, Mama. We're trying. You must be patient."

"How *can* I be? Three months already!"

When she asked Philip if he would like to have wine, milk, or soda water with his meal, Diana answered for him. "Water," she said, fearing the milk might not be sterilized.

"What does he speak? Does he speak your language?"

"No. He hasn't learned to speak yet."

"Not *yet*?"

"Well, he's only three years old. Some children start very late."

"Oh, really? Children here speak long before that."

"Not always, Mama," Lila offered. "I've heard of perfectly normal children who don't speak before three."

Señor Rossio's maiden sister Maria burst into the room and pulled up a chair, while his wife went scurrying into the kitchen and returned with a place setting for her. Tomás scowled and made room for her next to him at the table. She was a large, plain woman

"She's a fool!" replied Maria. "He comes from an old aristocratic family and thinks he doesn't have to work because of his name. And his looks."

"Well, at least he doesn't take his women from the town," her brother chuckled. "At least he has the decency to go to Buenos Aires to get them. I don't think she knows, do you, Maria?"

"Of course, she *knows*. But as long as he continues to return to her with roses and champagne, she'll go on forgiving. But she can't help it, I know. She's weak. Just like Mama was—"

Lila interrupted her aunt before she could go any further. "Papá tells me, don Miguel, you have brought the most fantastic machine with you that milks cows."

"Yes," her father answered for him. "Something we need here in this country. Perhaps, don Miguel, we can work together. I have the tools, the factory. You are the engineer. We cannot do anything right away, of course. Money is too tight, and José would never agree. But in the meantime, please believe my factory is at your disposal if you need to make spare parts, or anything like that."

As they were taking their leave, Lila looked worried. "Please," she said, taking Diana aside, "don't pay attention to my aunt. Maria is odd, but Papá adores her. She's been alone too much and been the boss for too long. She doesn't care what she says. She wasn't supposed to be here today. She just invited herself."

"Don't worry," Diana reassured her. "I understand."

"I do hope you will come again. Mama would like that. She needs company like you."

As they rode home Michael began to show interest in Señor Rossio's proposal. "If there were more machines like ours," he told Diana, "pasteurized milk could be sold on a commercial basis, and as Rossio said, cheese could qualify for export. Therefore, dairies could expect a higher price for their milk."

"Yes," she sleepily agreed, holding Philip close to her and staring out at the moonlit pampas. "They look like they are covered with milk. If you had your way, the whole world would be swimming in milk, wouldn't it?"

"No. I just want a *tambo*, a dairy, that can turn a profit. And a nice one at that!" Then he laughed. "What a strange family those Rossios."

"No. I understand them. Typical second- and third-generation immigrants. Concerned with money, status. Family. Maybe you

been safe in her arms, and the next he awoke to needles of pain in his mouth, tied down like an animal, and watched over by strangers ministering to him with instruments of torture.

His crying diminished slowly after three days, tears became sobs, silent sobs that made his chest heave. Diana had gripped the ledge of the glass window that separated her from her son, sobbing along with him, steeling herself from ripping open the door to his room, grabbing him, and running away.

She had endured two weeks of this hell alone, for Michael was only able to join her in the evenings. When the doctor declared that Philip was ready to go home, the nurse untied him, dressed him, and handed him to his parents. He did not know them. His eyes were glazed, expressionless. They were the eyes of a child who had already died. His arms hung like those of a rag doll by his sides. His legs did not work for him anymore. He had a palate, but they had lost their child.

Diana had kept him in her arms for three days and three nights. Rocking, singing, cooing, kissing. Willing him back to life. At the end of the fourth day, she dared set him down on the kitchen floor, where he had always liked to play. She lay next to him. He did not see her. But he saw Alex's water dish nearby, and a flicker of light wavered in the depths of his eyes, like a distant candle in the wind. He stared at it without moving. Then he slowly extended his hand. He touched it. He put his hand in the water. He looked up at Alex.

Then it happened. He smiled at Alex. Ever so carefully, he reached out and touched his fur. Alex trembled. Philip smiled again. Alex slowly waved his tail as Philip continued to lay his hand on him.

It was four hours later that he looked into his mother's eyes and remembered who she was. It took two more days before he was able to recognize his father.

"Anyway," Diana declared, "I think we should stick to just one language."

"All right," agreed Michael. "English is our native tongue. He'll learn Spanish soon enough from the others."

nal juices, he laughed. "She *does* like it."

Diana let out her breath. "That's all there is to it?"

"That's all."

Michael released the cow, but Bessie didn't want to leave, despite the open gate before her. "Why," he observed, giving her a slap on her rump to get her moving, "I think she wants more!"

The stunned cow slowly recovered herself and stumbled down the ramp. At the bottom she turned and looked back at them, as if in a trance, until she gradually seemed to realize who it was who had fucked her so well. She then bellowed with outrage before scurrying, her tail held high, out of the corral and into the fields.

Michael made Diana a chicken coop out of two large shipping crates, and when she went to the Montoyas to buy her chickens, the Señora appeared enormously relieved.

"Now," she told Diana, hugging and kissing her on the cheek, "you are almost a farmer's wife!"

Later Diana laughed with Michael. "Montoya might think I know a lot about farming, how to milk cows and raise calves, but I'm sure his wife knows that the only chickens I've ever cooked before are the kind you buy in the supermarket, and she wants to sell me a pair of turkeys, too. She says they would do well in the monte."

"By all means. I'd love to see turkeys in the monte."

With the arrival of spring, Michael turned over the former tenant farmer's corn field of sixty acres with the rotavator that had worked so well for the pastures in front of the casco. While he turned over the land, often with Philip on his lap and Alex running alongside the tractor, Rafael continued working on the construction of the dairy, and Diana decided the time had come for her to plant a vegetable garden.

Michael plowed the open space between the orchard and the monte for her. With the two white horses on the other side of the fence as occasional witnesses, she planted her first radishes, parsley, carrots, lettuce, spinach, and string beans, remembering how her father had done so in his little garden behind their house, not far in distance from New York City, yet, in time, a hundred years away. She remembered how, in the soft, scarlet summer twilight she and her father used to have their best—and really their only—talks together. Working now in her own garden she saw him clearly, as she

though with scissors. The plants bravely produced more leaves, but they, too, mysteriously disappeared. It could not be the work of a rabbit. The soil had not been disturbed, the surgery had been too perfect. There were no tracks of any kind left in the finely tilled earth, and there was no sign at all of any kind of insect. The same thing happened to the baby carrots and the beans. After the radishes had lost their third set of leaves, their tired stalks began to wither and die.

When the lettuce appeared, Diana watched the garden carefully but could not find a clue as to who was robbing her. One early morning, just after a rain, she discovered the lettuce half gone, cut down as surgically as had been the other plants. Throwing herself flat on the ground, she stared at the lettuce, as intently as a laboratory technician. Within minutes she noticed a little black ant making its way across the earth with a piece of lettuce on its back. The soil was so dark it was hard to spot the tiny creature. Soon, she found another and another ant doing the same thing. Advancing up the side of the carefully banked lettuce was a long column of them. They were methodically attacking the pale green baby leaves, cutting them quickly into a portable size and making off with them.

The column of thieves followed a path close to an oncoming column. On hands and knees, she traced these thieves all the way to the edge of the orchard, where they disappeared under the high grass.

"It's *ants*," she announced to Michael. "Ants!" and drove off to Las Rosas to get ant poison. She sprinkled the powder around the plants and all along the ants' line of march. It discouraged them somewhat, but still they kept on coming, stumbling over the poison until they decided to attack from a different direction.

Rafael caught her determinedly spreading more and more poison, and smiled, "The *cortedoras*. The cutting ants. You won't stop them like that. You must find their nests and put the poison inside it."

"How do you do that? The column goes on forever and then disappears."

"No. I will show you," he told her and parted the grasses in the orchard, peering down at the earth beneath. Their path could be seen very clearly, worn down, free of vegetation, as they hurried by the thousands back and forth from their nest to the vegetable garden. Dropping to hands and knees, Diana followed them, and when she finally came to the end of the path they made, she found only a

waved for forces both above and beneath the soil, laying before her a gift of great beauty.

Following instructions from *The Joy of Cooking* and remembering things her mother taught her, Diana made apricot and peach jam during the summer. Quince jelly and fig preserves. She canned as much fruit as she could get jars for and gave several away to Marlena Bauer, Señor Montoya, and the Berratos. Every evening Rafael carried a sack of fresh fruit back to his mother.

"Don't you think it's strange that people around here seem to think I know—or should know—everything about this place?" she asked Michael one day at lunch. "I mean, they never answer any questions. They just look away, or look at me queerly as though I *should* know and am only putting them on. Or trying to extract information from them they resent giving me for some reason.... Not Marlena, of course. She doesn't know anything about this place, and not much about farming, either. Nor Montoya's wife. I think she believes everyone else is wrong, and that I know nothing about farming at all. I can't fool her! Does Rafael ever say anything?"

"Nothing. You know he would never venture an opinion on anything. He has the true, laconic soul of the gaucho."

"I know. Still, it's so strange. Every morning, every time he arrives, he always looks at me surprised. As though to say, 'So, you are still here!'"

"I can understand that. You're not the sort of woman one expects to find in a tambo at six o'clock in the morning milking cows."

This was not what she meant, but she couldn't explain, even to Michael, that the way Rafael looked at her every morning haunted her. At first astonished, then puzzled, he searched her face for answers to unspoken questions.

tinue his slumber, Carlos poured Michael a scotch.

"Now that you've got all ten of your cows pregnant," he said, "you're soon going to be without milk. And since it's my fault, I'd like to propose a solution." He emptied his glass and poured himself another, topping off Michael's as well. "I'll go one better than Andrews. I'm prepared to sell you not ten but thirty cows. I've got a splendid lot, some ready to calve now, some within a month or two. What do you say?"

"Oh, that's generous of you but we couldn't afford thirty of the best of Southern Cross."

"Afford? You didn't let me finish. How about paying for ten within a year, ten the next, and ten the year after that? By that time a few of the heifers would amount to the payment, if indeed you'd be willing to part with them. What do you say?"

Diana drew in her breath. "That means increasing our herd by 300 percent—"

"That's right!" And he poured himself another scotch, filling Michael's glass as well.

"I'll drink to that," Michael said.

"Then it's settled?"

"Agreed!"

Raising his glass, he said, "To your campo!"

"To the Southern Cross!"

As Carlos poured himself a fourth scotch, Marlena looked at her husband pleadingly. When he refused to notice, her expression became one of tight-lipped resignation. Diana felt embarrassed for her and announced their departure. Marlena appeared relieved, whispering to her as she picked up the sleeping Philip, "Carlos should not drink. You must never let him drink. He can't handle it."

Diana realized she would have to drive home, but she didn't mind. It was the first time Michael had had a scotch since leaving London, and he had completely recovered by the time they reached their campo. After closing the gate, he took over the wheel and announced, "Now I am sure who Ernst really was."

"Carlos' cousin?"

"Yes. Ernesto. Chief of Staff of German Intelligence."

"How do you know?"

"Something Carlos said after you and Marlena left the room."

"Well, at least Carlos was not a Nazi."

the lone candle. A ghostly, dancing flame reflected like a distant signal in the old mirror on the other side of the room.

"But, you see, her captain, Langsdorf, believed that the whole British Navy was outside waiting for her. Oh, sure. He asked for instructions from Hitler, who told him to go out and *fight*. But he believed he hadn't a chance. So, at the end of the seventy-two hours, he put his officers and crew ashore, along with the British merchant seamen they had captured during their raids on British ships in the South Atlantic. Rather than risk having his ship fall into enemy hands, he sent it out with only a skeleton crew. To be scuttled. They followed their orders and sank the great ship. Only to find out that there was nothing out there but the three crippled cruisers, which returned to England, triumphant. The crews were marched in the streets of London as heroes. It wasn't a real victory for us, you understand. Just a victory of bluff. Langsdorf shot himself two days later."

Michael blew out the candle.

"Why? It wasn't his fault. It was a mistake."

"When you're a Captain, you don't make that kind of mistake. Shooting himself was the only honorable thing to do."

Diana was seized by a strange fear. Not of him, but for him. She said nothing. Instead, she asked, "And the crew? They came here?"

"Yes. To La Germania, the Tres Marias, Santa Clara, the Southern Cross. But not all. Some went back to Germany. Some stayed in Uruguay."

"I see...."

He climbed back into bed and settled himself down next to her, his body cold and rigid. She reached out, put her arm across his chest, and after a few minutes she felt him relax. "I think Carlos drinks a lot," she said.

"I don't blame him," he replied, adding, as he opened up his arms, drawing her close. "He's not in love with his wife, and that can be even worse than being a coward."

"She loves him."

"I know."

"Aren't we lucky?"

"Sh-hhh. Go to sleep."

Again, using the rotavator, Michael started turning over the entire eighty-acre parcel of their land that stretched from the dairy all the

hand-held machine Michael found for her in Rosario, similar to a meat grinder. Pleased with the results, she then proceeded to cover the entire casco's exterior uneven brick walls with stucco as well. She then painted the aged exterior window shutters a bright sapphire blue, which enhanced the tarnished silver blue-gray color of the newly stuccoed walls.

When completed, she took jasmine vines from the ruins of the house in the monte and planted them outside the new wall of the casco, where they flourished and soon covered the front of the former gallery, producing blossoms whose fragrance permeated the entire house when the picture windows were open, and could be inhaled from as far away as the ombú.

She discovered an unusual bushy shrub, similar to the nightblooming primrose, that she transplanted to the soil around the two doors Michael had placed at opposite ends of the former gallery, as well as around the old well outside the machine room. It was called the four o'clock plant because it bloomed precisely at four in the afternoon, producing great numbers of scarlet and white flowers, the size of wild roses. They bloomed all through the night, but with the coming of dawn the brilliant petals folded, slept through the day, and woke up once again with the approach of the setting sun.

Diana seeded the clearing in front of the casco with lawn grass and used the old bricks she retrieved from the ruins in the monte and from around the ombú to construct a walkway, whimsically meandering, from the roadside to the casco. Once in place, she bordered this path to her casco with colorful, variegated leaf croton plants also rescued from the monte.

She kept a fire going in the fireplace, day and night, for the rest of the winter. The warmth of the fireplace was especially welcome after a day in the fields. In the evenings Michael often fell asleep in his easy chair next to it while Diana shut off the noisy generator, preferring to read by candlelight on the couch before the comforting fire, Alex by her side. With the coming of dawn, Philip dashed from his cold room to huddle in front of it while Diana prepared hot chocolate milk for him. A fire in one's hearth on the pampas in winter is as welcome as the smile of one's beloved. It is a promise, and it is hope.

The monte supplied her with all the wood she needed. Once though, running short, Diana decided to gather some fallen dead branches from under the ombú. In the morning she found them intact. They had not burned along with the rest of the wood during

MARLENA came to visit Diana often, always bringing an assortment of her homemade delicacies, such as jars of glazed kumquats, marmalades, assorted pastries, sausages, and cheeses as well as *dulce de leche* for Philip, a thick, caramelized cream that the Argentine child consumes like the American child eats peanut butter.

One day when Michael was away, the usually reserved Marlena impulsively blurted out, without any warning, "I did my best. Before we were married I went to a doctor in Buenos Aires, and he assured me there was nothing wrong with me. There was no reason why I couldn't have children, even though I was in my thirties.

"But Carlos, of course...." She closed her eyes and finished in a whisper, "He never went to a doctor.... Now it's too late."

In the evening, after Philip had been put to bed, she continued her story. "I was a kindergarten teacher in Germany. Oh, yes, I have always taught children. Always loved them. When it was all...when it all happened in the beginning of the War, I was evacuated from Germany. Sent to Buenos Aires by the Baroness whose children I cared for at the time the Nazis took over."

Diana sat up, startled. "Yes," Marlena laughed softly. "Yes. I am Jewish. But no one knows that. Certainly not poor Agatha. Perhaps Ernesto does. I'm not sure. Only Carlos...and now you."

She did not wait for Diana's reply but went on with her story. "Carlos had been asked by the Baroness to look me up. To take care of me. She knew no one else here and remembered having done his family many favors. He found me in a small pensión, miserable and scared, I guess. Not able to speak Spanish. All alone. He felt sorry for me, I know. So he took me in. He took me here.

"Oh, don't worry. I have never regretted it. I'm not like Ernesto. I never want to go back. You see, I am from East Germany. Dresden. There is nothing left for me there now. My father was a professor. But they are dead now, my father and my mother. Killed by the Nazis, or maybe the Russians...who knows? And I was an only child."

"I'm sorry! How you must feel!"

"Yes. You can say it. A Nazi and a Jew. But don't worry. Please.

"All right," Diana agreed.

Once she was inside the dairy, though, the Duchess' doubting eyes became alive with interest, almost pleasure, although she didn't say much.

After Diana finished the milking, the Duchess explained: "I have heard about this place, and I want don Miguel to come and look over my dairy. Perhaps he can suggest what I might do to improve it. You could come, too, if you like. If he can spare you. I see you have no peón."

"Oh, yes, we do, but he has already gone for the evening."

"Why don't you come, say, next Friday? It's the Estancia San Juan near Correa, about ten kilometers south of Cañada de Gomez. You can ask there for directions. Anyone can tell you."

The Duchess then looked at Philip, standing next to Alex, and declared, "That is a beautiful dog."

"Thank you."

"And the boy? He is yours, too?"

"Why, yes."

"Bring him. While the Duke does not like children, I don't mind. Just for a visit. Our place is large enough, and he shouldn't get in the way."

Michael was pleased with the invitation. "Though Denitz warned us about her, remember? And Carlos, too. He told me to be careful. She's quite a business woman, and she knows how to squeeze a man's balls. Dry."

"Exactly who is she? Why is she here?"

"Carlos told me they came here after the War. To found a new empire, the Duke told him. But she's the one with the money. He is very strange. She runs the estancia entirely. Rides as well as a gaucho and even has been known to rope and brand cattle herself."

The Duchess was right. They had no difficulty finding Estancia San Juan. It was the largest landholding in the countryside south of Cañada de Gomez and north of Casilda, and San Juan's monte could be seen from a considerable distance. A tall, intricately worked wrought-iron gate was at the entrance to the driveway, which wound for half a mile through carefully planted woods. Eucalyptus lined the road, giving way to a canopy of palm trees. They passed hundreds of them before reaching the main house.

"Goodness!" Diana drew in her breath as she caught sight of it.

"Yes. Of course. Frederick, you can take Diana on a tour of the house and gardens while we are gone. And we will take the boy with us."

The Duke appeared relieved. "Fine. You see, Madame, there are so many precious things of great historical value inside that a little boy could break."

"Really?" she queried, raising her eyebrows.

"Quite by accident, of course, but still it's possible. I cannot tell you what a work it was to bring everything over from Europe. It took me almost two years! So you see, I cannot take any chances, you understand."

"Of course." Though annoyed, Diana smiled politely. "Philip shall go with his father."

"And," the Duchess added, "if you are lucky, Frederick might even tell you your fortune."

"I don't tell fortunes," he replied, not looking at his wife. "I do horoscopes. But, of course, there will be no time for that today."

There was a minute of loud silence, as though the Duke and Duchess were momentarily retreating to gather more ammunition with which to wound one another. It was obvious the Duchess had nothing but scorn for her husband, and he was clearly afraid of her.

Glancing over at the chateau, Diana volunteered, "It's pink."

"Yes," the Duchess agreed. "I had it painted that way. Reminds me of the Mediterranean. A folly of mine, I know, and Frederick doesn't approve."

She turned back to Michael as two maids dressed in white lace-trimmed aprons and caps passed silver platters of petits fours. A butler in white gloves came forward to serve the tea. The roughened hands of the girls identified them as local farm folk, whereas the butler was obviously not from the area. The Duchess did not remove her hat throughout the ceremony, and the thought occurred to Diana that she might be bald.

When she had finished her tea, the Duchess got up from the table. "Let's go now," she said to Michael, and started off across the lawn. He rose to follow, smiling at Diana. The Duke immediately rose as well, and offering Diana his arm, asked, "Won't you come with me, Madame?"

She nodded. Michael took Philip's hand and turned to where the Duchess was waiting for him.

The tour began with the gardens. The Duke explained that the estancia had once belonged to an old Spanish family whose sons

This appeared to anger him, and he began to complain about the ineptitude of his gardeners. "Just look at the state of that water! I have paid thousands for new pumps, replaced miles of old pipes, and still they cannot keep decent water in these canals!"

He directed her back along a path towards the chateau. "Let me show you the house now." Across from the lawns, facing the chateau, was an Olympic-sized swimming pool. It was empty.

"It's useless," the Duke announced. "I forgot to drain it last winter when my wife was in Europe and it froze. She's still angry about it. I read a lot, you see, and I just simply forgot about it. Come! Let me show you my library." He was smiling again.

The Duke led Diana through room after room of silent grandeur. "After the War I couldn't afford to live in the castle anymore," he told her. "So I decided to take all this to another country. To *save* it, you see. And Argentina seemed—at the time—like the best place. Although, I often wonder if I made the right choice. Perhaps Canada…but my wife couldn't have stood the cold."

He sounded lonely, and looked as though he were lost.

"My brother preferred to live in the gatekeeper's cottage. I suppose he's happy there, but I couldn't do that. I had the responsibility of *preserving*." His eyes lost their self-assurance and pleaded for understanding.

"Yes," she gently reassured him, "I know."

There was a faint odor of mildew everywhere, even though several windows were opened to the warm dry air outside the chateau. The Duke was an exile who had surrounded himself with mountains of memories.

The dining hall was a great circular room, a separate building, constructed in the center of the chateau's inner courtyard. It was dark inside. Black velvet drapes had been drawn across the many windows set into its round walls. The Duke flicked a light switch, illuminating several large crystal chandeliers that hung from the ceiling in a circle above an enormous round oak table capable of seating fifty people. Incredibly, this table was set with fine china, crystal, and gleaming silver. All that was missing were the guests.

The Duke's library was the only room that appeared to be lived in. "I spend all my time here," he said. "It contains 10,000 volumes that I have catalogued myself. You might say it's my life's work."

His bedroom adjoined the library, and books were piled high on the tables on both sides of his canopied bed, on the floor, and more peeked out from under the bed. There were books on the

XVI desk. "I flew over only briefly to sign the papers and then returned to Europe to arrange for the shipping. I had to be very careful, you understand. The timing had to be right. All the signs had to be favorable. Finally, the ship was chosen. But on the morning set for loading, I woke up to discover it was all wrong. I had made a terrible mistake. My horoscope predicted not favorable conditions but disaster. You know," he confided, "horoscopes can be extremely tricky. So I rushed down to that quay in Hamburg and stopped everything. I warned the captain, but of course he didn't—couldn't—listen. So the ship sailed, but without our fortune, and was hit by a freak storm off the Canary Islands. Broke in two. And sank." His hand shook as he wiped his brow and several moments passed before he was able to recover from the memory of the terrible calamity he had managed to avoid.

He then continued, "I had to wait three more months before the signs were indeed in my favor again and it was safe to let my children...." His eyes roamed over the thousands of volumes covering the paneled walls—some locked securely behind glass doors. "To let my children," he went on, "leave Europe. I traveled with them, of course."

"One could spend a lifetime in this room," Diana told him, wistfully. "I, too, brought many books. I could not live without them."

Outside a child was laughing.

"They have returned," the Duke announced and, rising from his carved and gilded armchair, he followed Diana out onto the lawn.

Just before she bid her host and hostess good-bye, the Duke told Diana loudly enough for everyone to hear, "Come and see me again. I don't go away often anymore. It is rare I even get to Buenos Aires. I used to go when there was a good book fair. I have been known, you see, to travel anywhere in the world for an auction of rare books. Now they don't tempt me as much as before. And dealers send me catalogs directly. I urge my friends to visit me, but," he shrugged, "even those in Buenos Aires come rarely. They tell me they don't have the time. And Buenos Aires is so close...."

As he pressed her hand to his lips their eyes met. Such a lonely man, Diana thought, and felt infinitely grateful for the son who was turning somersaults on the lawn waiting for his parents to take him home, and for the handsome man next to her who was enthusiastically discussing plans for a new dairy with an admiring Duchess.

AS the wheat grew, so did Philip. But it grew faster than the boy, and by the time it was the color of champagne, like his hair, he could lose himself in it, which he loved to do. However, Diana always knew where he was by searching the fields for the tip of Alex's tail that was also the same color as the wheat but did not wave gently with the wind as did the golden stalks of grain. It shook rapidly back and forth. If she thought Philip was getting too far away, she could call Alex with a special high-pitched whistle Michael had brought back from one of his trips to Buenos Aires, and Alex would nudge Philip homeward.

Once the whistle so startled Alex he turned and dashed back toward the casco without warning Philip. When he realized what he had done, he ran back to where he thought he had left the boy, but Philip had gone on, and Alex could not find him in the dense growth. The wheat was a solid wall of vegetation, covering natural grasses which had sprung up between the rows in the previously virgin field.

When Diana realized what all the barking was about, she too plunged into the field, calling for him. Philip had already gone a considerable distance from the house when she had first called Alex, and she struggled through the field as fast as she could to reach the spot where she thought she had first seen her dog. By the time she reached it, calling out for Philip all the way, her heart was pounding, perspiration running down her face. But her sweat dried cold as she scanned the great field and could see no sign of her son in the sea of rippling flaxen waves rolling towards her from the edge of the horizon, like a gentle tide coming in.

Again and again, she shouted his name, "Philip! Philip! Answer me! Why don't you answer me? Show me where you are? Philip! Oh, God, *Philip*!" she cried, desperate, full of fear.

Over and over she continued to plead. Nothing answered her calls but the silence of the land. Alex stopped his wild barking as he stood tense, his ears twitching for a signal of some kind from the lost boy. But the only sound they could hear was the whisper of the southerly wind as it rustled through the grain. And in the distance, on the other side of the campo, the monotonous drone of Michael

move. As she reached out for him, he jumped up, startled to see her there. When she held him high for Michael to see and covered him with her kisses and tears of exultation, she was filled with a new kind of horror.

She waited until evening to tell Michael. As she watched Philip run from her to his father to kiss him good night, she said softly, "I think our son is deaf."

Michael laughed. "Nonsense! He hears everything I say."

"Test him. Try calling him from behind, where he can't see you. Where he can't see your lips."

As Philip stopped at the door of his bedroom to pet Alex, Michael called to him. The boy didn't turn around. Michael went closer, knelt down behind Philip's ear and called again, softly at first, then louder and louder until he was almost shouting.

"Stop it!" Diana cried out.

Philip turned and looked up, perplexed, at the frightened faces of his parents.

"Now we know why he hasn't spoken yet. Take him to the doctor in the morning," Michael told her, his tanned face suddenly gray and drawn.

Later in bed, he was more hopeful. "It could be just something temporary, you know. I can't believe he has *never* heard me. Perhaps it's just a cold. Sometimes these things can be cleared up."

"But he doesn't have a cold."

"Sometimes these conditions just go away by themselves. I've known that to happen to divers, for instance. They go down too far, and *wham* the pressure is too much, and they can lose their hearing. Or it can even happen at depths they are used to. It's rare, but it can happen. No one knows exactly why. And then, just as inexplicably, their hearing returns. But it takes time."

An elderly woman waited with Diana and Philip in the austere anteroom of the only doctor in Las Rosas. Well dressed, her hair recently waved, she was obviously one of the town's more prosperous inhabitants, though Diana had never seen her before. She had looked up at Diana, startled, when they came in, and now sat staring at her from across the room in one of the four massive ladder-back oak armchairs that were the room's sole furnishings. She sat straight up, as stiffly as if she had a rod in her spine, and she continued to stare at Diana with intense interest. When she finally spoke, it was not to Diana, but to an invisible companion, saying, "I think

mind. It's not important. Let me know what the specialist in Buenos Aires has to say. Then come back to me if I can do anything more." He bowed and opened the door for her.

"Yes," she nodded numbly, not knowing what more to say, and passed into the antechamber where the old woman still sat, waiting. As Diana opened the door to the street, their eyes met once again, and the woman stared at her with the same fearful look as before.

After dinner Michael told Diana, "I'm going to saddle Mora and check on the herd. There's one I think is about to calve."

He was gone for a long time. Diana lay in bed hoping for sleep despite the thoughts tormenting her. She remembered the last meeting she had with the plastic surgeon who had closed Philip's upper lip when he was ten days old, after everyone, except Diana, had given up hope he would live. The cleft in his face was so extreme, the hospital in England had simply put him in a private room with his mother and, unable to nurse, expected her to feed Philip formula with a spoon. Within three days he had lost three pounds. Diana had to scream for help, demanding to see the American ambassador, before a surgeon was found who agreed to perform the operation enabling Philip to suck normally from a nipple.

After the operation the surgeon had told her, "I must warn you that his kind of cleft lip and palate is just the tip of the iceberg. Underneath can lie many problems. Problems that will surface with time, one by one...."

Diana got up and went out in her robe into the summer night to look for Michael. First, she went toward the ombú, hoping from that elevated point to see the horse and its rider somewhere in the moonlight. Instead, she found him standing under the tree.

"Do we deserve this?" he asked, without looking at her.

"No."

She tried to put her arms around him, but he drew away.

Turning around, taking her by the shoulders, he told her, "We must see that he gets the best. The best doctors in the country. *In the world.*"

The ear specialist in Buenos Aires repeated almost word for word what the old country doctor had told her. There was nothing to be done for Philip except wait and hope that his ears would clear up by themselves. "Perhaps, while you are here, you should also see a plastic surgeon. You will soon need to take care of his face."

She and Philip visited the surgeon he recommended. The man

vitality about them that was unmistakably different from the young people of Las Rosas. As she drank her strong coffee, and Philip his boiled milk, eating the ubiquitous ham sandwiches found in every café in Argentina, she overheard the name Perón mentioned several times. As a result of the incident on the bus, she now knew it was a name which could only be whispered in public. If the military regime was ever to be defeated and democracy restored, if any real change was ever to come to the country, she suspected it would begin in Córdoba.

The ear specialist was not any more helpful than the one in Buenos Aires, and the plastic surgeon he sent her to had never done the operation Philip would need. "But, Señora, I would be willing to try. I've seen it done in New York."

After speaking with him Diana made up her mind to take Philip to New York. To where all these so-called specialists had received their training. And decided while she was in Córdoba to have her and Philip's U.S. passports renewed. It was the only consulate outside of Buenos Aires.

The Consul General was surprised to meet her, telling her, "You are the only U.S. citizen, a woman, to own land here. Sure, there are a few other women from the States here, mostly from Texas, but they are married to Argentine estancieros."

"I'm going back for him," she said.

The Consul looked at Philip carefully. "I understand. You are right to do so."

Michael wasn't worried about money when she explained how she felt. "I told you. I promised you he shall have nothing but the best," he assured her. "We need only wait for the wheat."

"Come where?" She had never seen the child before.

"To my house," the little one answered. "I've been waiting here for you all week. But I knew you would come today. I told them it *had* to be today. And I was right!" she cried, starting forward.

Diana hesitated. "It's just down there, my house. Come!" the child insisted and began walking, leaving Diana no choice but to follow.

Only tradespeople lived along the block near the post office, and Diana didn't know any of them. About halfway down the street, lined with one long series of dismal two-story buildings, some with great gaping cracks snaking across their gray facades, Diana saw a severe-looking woman, dressed in black, standing beside an open door. When Diana and Philip reached her, the little girl said, "This is my mother," and slipped past her into the house.

It was the home and shop of the village tailor. Whenever Diana had passed this house on her way to the central plaza, she could see him through the open door, working at his table.

Now, before she had a chance to say anything, the little girl's mother hissed, "Come quick!" The moment they entered the little vestibule, the woman shut the door, latching it as well.

Diana found herself in a small, dark room, well shuttered against the bright morning sun, where several people were gathered around the tailor's large, circular table, looking like mourners.

"*Buenos días,*" she said brightly. But no one in the grave group returned her greeting.

"Sit down," the child's mother told her. After she had done so, with Philip pressed against her side, the woman withdrew a letter from the pocket of her dress and placed it on the table before her. "Please, tell us what it says," she asked, sitting down next to her, clasping her hands together on the table, trying to control her anxiety.

The man opposite Diana was the tailor. He stared at her, his eyes filled with dread. An old woman, undoubtedly the grandmother, sat beside him.

On Diana's left was an attractive young woman, dressed in the traditional white smock worn by the elementary school teachers of Las Rosas. She flashed Diana a brief, nervous smile and introduced herself as the tailor's daughter and the man sitting next to her as her husband. He nodded, then glanced quickly away.

The entire family continued to regard Diana in silence, waiting. She picked up the envelope and observed, "It's from Canada."

band left her and little Eric. Eric is fine now; although, he has been sick. But he is wild sometimes, and Marta, because her mind is not well, cannot control him."

"Ah...!" the mother gasped, "What does that mean? Her mind? What does he mean?"

"I don't know," Diana answered. "Let me see."

She felt her hands becoming moist. Her Argentine Spanish was far from perfect, and she knew she must find the right words to explain what the priest was trying to say.

"It's a small town," the priest wrote. Diana hesitated before the next sentence, and her voice trembled when she finally was able to continue translating, *"and I know that Marta has tried to commit suicide twice."*

But no one reacted. "Go on," the mother murmured sadly.

"She tried to get a job, but Marta speaks very little English and has no experience. People here have no money for maids or anything like that which she could do. Finally, though, she did get a job, part-time, in the beauty parlor. She put Eric in a nursery, but after six months he became very ill and was in the hospital for two months.

"Now you must know Marta is a good mother. And when Eric was sick, she went crazy with worry. Understand, being all alone, and with no money, it was difficult. She quit her job because she had to be with him to nurse him back to health. Now, she worries about him all the time."

Diana looked up to see tears flowing down the face of the grandmother who, up to this point, had remained emotionless and silent.

"My housekeeper," the priest continued, *"found her six months ago, crying in the church. She was starving and cold. Now Marta is always cold, which I do not understand. And she keeps saying she hasn't enough to eat. This, too, I do not understand. I really do try to feed her well. But she remains thin. Now she won't eat at all—"*

"Ayeeeeeee!" the mother wailed. The father stared at Diana, horrified, as though he could not believe what she was telling them, and the little girl who had brought her stood gravely immobile behind her mother's chair. Even Philip, always restless, did not move, hypnotized by the drama being played out around him.

"But please, continue," the mother begged, as she sobbed without shame now.

There wasn't much more to read. The unhappy priest ended his letter saying, *"I really don't know what's to become of her. She talks only of you and Argentina. How beautiful it is and how warm and how every-*

back. It is all right," she quietly announced.

"Yes," the mother said. "We must have our grandson."

Diana rose to go.

"Wait. Wait a minute," the mother asked, "and I will show you a picture of him."

She disappeared into a back room and returned with a framed color photograph of a handsome little blond boy about Philip's age. She smiled proudly, almost in control again.

"He is beautiful," Diana assured her.

Then the woman grabbed both of Diana's hands in hers and, kissing her on both cheeks, murmured, "Thank you, Señora. Thank you. God will bless you. And God will take care of *your* boy, too."

These words brought quick, grateful tears to Diana's eyes.

Marta's sister accompanied her to the pickup. It was almost noon, and the crowds of shoppers had thinned out in front of the post office. Stopping before the truck, the teacher took her hand and, holding it tightly in hers, asked for assurance. "You won't say anything, will you?" she begged, looking about her at the few old women left on the streets, shopping bags in hand, heading home after making their daily rounds of the shops to gossip and buy the day's provisions. "They are all so mean."

"I understand."

"It will be hard enough for her *without* them knowing. Oh, poor Marta! We were never good enough for her. She always wanted to go to the big city—and now! I, too, have children. What about them? What if the Directrice of my school ever finds out? And my husband's business? We could be ruined."

Las Rosas suddenly lost all its quaintness for Diana, its alluring strangeness. It was a trap, and she was glad to be considered to be apart from it. To be "from the *outside*."

"Of course," Diana reassured her once again. "Don't worry."

Michael was waiting for her when she returned home. "Where have you been? I need to go to the Southern Cross for semen."

Diana told him about the letter. "Please ask Carlos about this fellow. He used to work for him."

"I'll see what I can do," he promised.

When he returned, Michael reported that Carlos had answered him, "'Oh, *that* one! A real son of a bitch.' He told me he was sent out to him from Germany, and he doesn't even know by whom. A friend of a friend, he guesses, who thought maybe he could

A S the time approached to harvest their wheat, they prayed that it would not rain, and especially that it would not hail. "It's pampero season," Michael worried. "At this time of year it comes with hail, too, and hail would break the backs of the slender stalks. They are already bending under the weight of the ripened grain, and if the grain were to fall now, it would rot, and we would lose everything."

Insurance against hail or crop failure did not exist for the small farmer. The great estancieros' insurance was the very vastness of their land and financial reserves accumulated over generations. Farming here is like a lottery, Diana decided, looking up at the sky. And it's you, God, who holds the winning ticket. Every time a threatening cloud rose up from the south, she begged the wind to carry it away.

"But what I'm really worried about are the winds from the north," Michael told Diana. "Talk in Las Rosas is that we're over-due for such a storm. They get one here about every twenty years and it's been longer than that since one has hit."

"Is it like a tornado, a twister?" Diana wondered.

"No. Worse. More like a cyclone. But without rain."

"That's the kind of storm," she remembered, "the tenant farmer who was here two years ago warned me about. The kind of wind that can drive one crazy if it blows for more than three days."

"It can do more than drive you crazy! If it ever comes, I want you and Philip to get under this table." They were having breakfast. "That would be the safest place. The casco has survived these storms so far...."

The following morning just before the dawn when the stars were being extinguished, one by one, by the approaching sun, they heard a rumbling on the high road. In the distance several harvest-ers appeared on the hazy horizon, advancing in single file like a fleet of battleships.

"They are harvesting at Santa Clara," Michael announced, and there was awe in his voice. "It has begun."

The machines had been lying in wait in Las Rosas for two weeks. They had come from all over the country, each with a different owner, a different crew who had spent the waiting time cleaning, oiling, repairing, making everything shipshape for the oncoming assault and race against the weather.

As they watched them advance out of the mist, heading south to Santa Clara, they wondered what everyone else was asking themselves and what would be the talk of Las Rosas that night. How many tons per acre would the Admiral get? Santa Clara had more than 50,000 acres under wheat this year and had to plant earlier than anyone else in order to finish the harvest before the weather turned against them.

"There is going to be much excitement in Las Rosas tonight," Michael said, taking Diana's hand. "The cafés will be full. The harvest at Santa Clara is like the opening of a London play and there, heading south, go the critics."

"I hope it will be a good review."

But it was not. It had not rained enough, and Santa Clara harvested barely a ton an acre. Yet, as the other estancieros and smaller farmers in the area drank their wine that night, Michael reported back to Diana, "They boasted they had a right to hope for more from their land than the Admiral got. For one reason or another."

Michael's harvest was agonizingly delayed because, being a newcomer, he was last on the list for a harvester. But the weather held, and his machines finally arrived to maneuver, like ships in battle, across their campo, slashing away at the grain all day long under a threatening sky. Sounds of their rumbling and throbbing as they ate up the wheat continued far into the night when they continued to search out their prey with blinding lights. They stopped only when the morning dew forced them to. After a quick breakfast of bread and meat, washed down with maté, the crew returned to their machines to set sail once again as soon as the sun had burned off the morning mists.

When the men had finished, they left behind them not the usual dry brown stubble, but rather a field of green dotted here and there with small hills of burlap sacks. The stubble was there, but it was hidden among the new grass that had been lying in wait for its chance in the sun. Diana stood with Philip under the ombú and watched the ships fade away, until there was nothing left to see but a trail of smoke on the horizon.

Exhausted, covered with soot and stubble, Michael lifted Diana high in the air when he joined her under the ombú and swung her around. "Almost three tons an acre! Our first wheat, and we have

the paraiso trees falling all about him. When he managed to force open the gate against the wind, most of the cows wouldn't move. They were paralyzed with fear, and he had to beat them out into the open field where they would be safe from the falling trees and flying roofing which whizzed through the air like swords. One after the other, the great eucalyptuses in the corral fell, and the largest one near the casco split right down the middle, as though sliced through with a great knife, before going down.

Crouching low, Diana pushed against the wind to reach the stall where she had left Philip. When she got there, she was horrified. He was not there, nor was Alex. She screamed, but her screams were only a whimper in the face of the wind roaring around, about, and above her. Michael found Diana hysterical. "I can't find him! He's not where I told him to stay! Nor is Alex!"

"Maybe in the house!"

"Impossible! He could never have gotten out in time!" For the path to the casco had been blocked by fallen trees within minutes after the winds had hit.

To get around the fallen trees they had to go out into the fields where they had harvested the wheat and approach the casco from the south, their bodies doubled in half as they tried to keep from being blown off their feet. "Get down!" warned Michael. "Must be over a hundred miles an hour. I know this kind of wind."

They were finally forced to crawl on their hands and knees as they got closer to the house.

Diana was shaking as she reached for the handle of the front door, sure she wouldn't find Philip inside, and yet not knowing what she would do if he were not there.

But he was. Under the kitchen table, hugging Alex. Both boy and dog were trembling.

He crawled out, throwing his arms open to clasp her neck, and sobbed in her embrace. "Darrrling!" he said. The sound was like that of someone being rescued from the grave.

Diana danced wildly with him in her arms around the room. "Darling! Darling! Darling! You can speak!"

Philip slid from her arms, as astonished as she, repeating the strange sounds which had just escaped from his lips. "Darrrling! Darrrling! Darrrling!"

"And all the while I've been trying to teach him 'Mommy'!"

"Of course. It's logical," Michael answered, taking his son into his arms, and he, too, covered him with kisses. "Why should he call

tered with broken branches, with profound gratitude and understood why the casco had been built like a fort. It was not only for protection against the Indians but also against the treacherous winds of the pampas. Whereas the roof of the dairy had been lifted off as easily as a cover on a pot by the hand of the furious storm.

Though she knew it would take months of work to repair the destruction, she could feel no real despair as they surveyed the damage. The only sound she could hear was that of her son's first word. It kept exploding in her ears. "Darrrling! Darrrling!"

Michael, too, only shrugged at the destruction, holding his son close. "We will build again," he said.

how to use makeup well, it still couldn't hide the hollowed-out cheek bones, and the dark circles beneath her large, sad eyes.

"Las Rosas! So primitive!" she laughed, with some scorn.

When they reached the dirt road, Marta was jolted almost to the roof of the pickup from the shock of leaving the highway.

"Really!" she exclaimed. "How can you stand it? I mean, I *know* what kind of roads you have in New York. Why, in Ontario such a road as this could not be found. Not as a main road, anyway. And the people here. How can you stand them? So backward! And the crazy things they say about your campo! Do you know?" she asked, turning her eyes from the dusty red road to focus on Diana. "My grandmother didn't want me to come. She says your place is haunted."

"Oh, no." Diana shook her head, keeping her eyes on the road. "It's the place across the way."

Marta frowned, then went on. "Of course it's good for Eric. To know his grandparents. Mama has been so anxious to see him. That's why I agreed to return, but just for a visit, of course."

"Of course," Diana said, mildly surprised at the game she was playing. Surely, she thought, they told her it was I who translated the letter. Then, maybe they didn't. Maybe they never even told her about the letter. And that's the real reason the grandmother didn't want her to come. Afraid I might say something.

Marta's eyes widened when she saw Michael and she blushed deeply as he shook her hand. Alex greeted them too, sniffing at Eric and trying gently to play with him, but the little boy screeched with fear, quickly escaping into the casco.

Diana urged Philip, "Show Eric your toys." After a short time, he emerged from Philip's room with a box of building blocks, put them on the floor and stared at them. Diana went into the kitchen to prepare tea, and when she returned with the tea tray, he had begun to build a house. "How pretty!" she exclaimed. He glowered up at her and then smashed everything he had just made.

"Sometimes he doesn't feel well," Marta explained, her voice bright but brittle, as though it were about to break as had the house of blocks.

As the afternoon wore on, Marta chattered incessantly. She insisted upon recounting the glamorous life she had had in Canada, telling Diana and Michael what a sacrifice it had been to return, "Just to please Mama, of course."

According to her account, her family had forced her to come back, and she hadn't wanted to. She had been happy in Canada.

not want to deepen their relationship any further. That perhaps Diana already knew her too well.

"It was nice, anyway," Diana told Michael when she returned. "Eric was frightened, I think."

"No. He is merely spoiled."

"He liked you. She did, too. I could tell."

"You should try to help her more. Have her here more often. Imagine, taking a girl like that to Canada!"

Diana abruptly turned on him. "Imagine taking a girl like me to Las Rosas!" The bitterness in her voice surprised her, and she was ashamed of herself.

"You want to go back, don't you?"

"Yes! No. Oh, just for a visit. There is a loneliness some-times…. Oh, God!" She moaned and ran out into the twilight. And started to cry under the ombú, not understanding exactly why.

The next time Diana saw Marta she looked considerably older, her features haggard and pinched, despite her makeup. She stood on a street corner, helplessly pleading with Eric to stop fighting with two other boys. She was embarrassed to see Diana and, at first, turned away.

"How are you?" Diana quietly asked. For a moment Marta didn't answer. "It's very hard…." She stammered, starting to cry. "I tried to get a job in Rosario but without schooling, I can't. And I don't have any money for school."

"Perhaps you could get a bank loan."

"Oh, no! Never. They would never give it to *me*."

"It couldn't hurt to at least talk to the bank manager. If he can't help himself, maybe he can direct you to somewhere else. Try," Diana urged. "Do try. And don't forget to look your prettiest when you go to see him," she added, as she walked away.

That evening Carlos Bauer stopped by the campo on his way back from Santa Clara to see Michael. Diana recounted her meet-ing with Marta and explained what was happening to her. "It's such a pity."

"Yes," Carlos agreed and said nothing more. However, before leaving, when Michael had already gone out into the night, he took her hand, and holding it tightly in his for a brief moment, he qui-etly said, "I'll talk to the bank manager. God knows without me and the Southern Cross that son of a *puta* would be counting pesos somewhere in the Chaco Desert."

MARLENA Bauer was waiting for Diana when she pulled up to the side entrance of the house of the Southern Cross. Carlos was there in the kitchen having a cup of coffee, but when he saw her, he put the cup down, got up, and walked past her with only a nod.

"Aren't you even going to say hello to Philip?" Marlena asked.

But he was already out the door, down the steps, and did not look back.

Marlena frowned. She stood in the doorway, and her eyes filled with tears as they followed Carlos heading for his office down the road.

"He didn't hear you," Diana offered.

Marlena smiled briefly like someone who is ill. But almost immediately the mask of circumspection, which she habitually wore, returned to shield her real feelings.

Diana realized that for a long time now Carlos had been avoiding her. He was always too busy to come to dinner at her house. Whenever Marlena invited her to the Southern Cross, he drank heavily with Michael, sometimes toasting her as "The Happiness Kid," with an edge of bitterness in his voice, and would quickly look away whenever their eyes chanced to meet.

Diana followed Marlena down the hall toward the living room.

"Agatha is joining us for lunch," she whispered before opening the door. "Ernesto isn't feeling well, and Agatha thought he'd do better here. Although, I doubt it." She shook her head. "He doesn't like the country. Says it doesn't agree with his ulcers. Or his asthma. Poor Agatha." She shook her head again. "Carlos' cousin is not an easy man."

Agatha was sitting next to the fireplace, an open book on her lap. "Yes," she said, her pale eyes filming over as Diana expressed her concern for Ernesto. "I thought it would do him good to come to the Tres Marias, but I was wrong. We shall be returning to Buenos Aires next week. Perhaps you can come to stay with us? For a visit? You and Philip? You certainly deserve a vacation. Or maybe even to Villa Gesell? We have a vacation house there on the beach. You'd be most welcome."

Agatha signed. "That is Ernesto's trouble. He can never get used to this...." Her arm swept over the land, as she looked toward that point where the blue and white sky met the broad green earth. "Ah!" she turned back to face Diana. "But it's not the same for you. You can go back. We cannot. Oh, my beloved country.... The homesickness is terrible. Not for me, you understand. But it's killing Ernesto."

Three months later Diana received a letter from Agatha, announcing that Ernesto was being granted, on humanitarian grounds, a visa to return for a short visit to his castle in Bavaria, where his ninety-year-old mother lay dying. She had requested to see her son one last time. "After all," Agatha wrote, "it has been twenty years. They can no longer deny him this right."

Agatha invited Diana to stay with her for the two weeks Ernesto would be away. "Meet me in Buenos Aires where we have to go to complete a monumental pile of documents before he can leave. Then we will drive together down to Villa Gesell and enjoy the beach together! *Please.* You and Philip must come. I should die of suspense wondering about Ernesto all by myself."

Diana's instinct was to refuse. She never felt quite comfortable in Agatha's presence, as she did with Marlena. And two whole weeks alone with her? In the home of a German officer who had most likely been convicted of war crimes?

But the idea of giving Philip the chance to see the ocean, to play in the sand, was tempting. Michael urged her to go. The vacation would do everyone good. "I can manage with Rafael," he assured her.

"But if you can't, if you need me, will you send for me? Send a telegram?"

"I doubt if that will be necessary. Think what good relations you can establish for us. Carlos has done a lot, but Ernesto could do far more. And don't let your conscience bother you. Ernesto belongs to the aristocracy. The old guard. Officers like him never had anything to do with Hitler."

Diana decided to go directly by bus to the seaside resort of Villa Gesell. Agatha was proud to show her the town. "It is Ernst who designed most of the homes here for our countrymen. It is he who has laid out the design of Villa Gesell."

"It's incredible. One would not believe one was in Argentina! It

fire. Nero fiddling while Rome burned. Then back at Agatha's smile.

She put her knitting aside. "There was no question that we would escape. Each officer had a plan worked out. Ernst sent me down to Bavaria. It never received much damage, you know. As though both sides had agreed to keep it safe. A haven. A place to escape to. A base to rebuild from. *But I didn't want to leave.* We had only recently been married, and it had been so long, so hard, for him to get his divorce. You see, I am only Ernst's second wife."

"Oh?"

"Yes. Before, I had been his secretary."

She stood up, plucked a yellow rose from the bowl on the coffee table, and caressed her cheek with the flower. "I finally agreed to go, just two days before you Americans entered Berlin. Ernst sent me to his mother's castle in Bavaria, in the mountains, not far from Switzerland. Along with his first wife, and his daughter, of course. The next day he himself left. Only *then* did I worry."

Agatha's eyes widened, bright and clear. The happiness replaced by the memory of fear.

"The roads were closed or torn up, and the chauffeur almost didn't make it. He had to make detours, zigzag across fields. It took them three days. Oh, *that* was the bad time for me. That was the difficult time. I was so frightened. When the limousine finally arrived, it was in the middle of the night, and it was full of bullet holes. Of course, you see, Ernst had to remain to the last. He was not an important official, you understand. He just felt it was his duty to do so."

"Yes, of course."

In the morning, while walking on the windswept beach with Philip between them, Agatha said, "Perhaps you don't know this, but when Argentina realized Germany was going to lose the war, they suddenly declared war on us. Just before the end. We never really had any idea of coming here. Ernst was not a Nazi. We knew they would never try him for war crimes, or anything like that. But when Argentina declared war, they also issued a decree saying that all property which belonged to Germans who were not in the country within thirty days, or something like that, if they were not here, it would be confiscated. So we *had* to come.

"Carlos sent our lawyer to meet us at the Swiss border. And you know, we had to *walk* all the way. All the way from the castle to the Swiss border. Carrying our suitcases through the snow. Oh, I didn't

"Of course. But what will I do?"

"Perhaps Marlena can come down and stay with you?"

"No. No. Not Marlena. I'll get one of my friends here to come."

When Diana told Michael what had happened he said, "How can you be so naive?"

"How can *you* do business with them?"

"Oh, Diana, you don't know what you are saying. Grow up!"

"We could work with Andrews. He's English. And Denitz. He's half English."

"I can't afford them. Besides, they don't have the resources that Carlos has."

"What about the Duchess?"

"She's too far away."

"But, God, Michael. Your own mother killed by the Germans!"

"And don't you think I've killed a few myself?"

"What do you mean?"

"Oh, Diana." He gripped her shoulders. His eyes stabbed like knives into hers. "You don't know what it was like! During the invasion having to go from house to house, tree to tree. Hoping against hope there wasn't a German hiding behind one that I would have to shoot in the face. Point blank. They were only boys then by the end of the war. Fifteen. Sixteen. Only boys were left. *You don't know what it was like.*"

~ Part III ~
A Gaucho Born and Bred

Son am I of the rolling plain,
A gaucho born and bred,
For me the whole great world is small,
Believe me, my heart can hold it all…

I was born on the mighty pampas' breast,
As the fish is born in the sea,
And this is my pride: to live as free
As the bird that cleaves the sky…

Martín Fierro, by José Hernández

~

HEN construction on the farm was completed, when order had been restored to the corral and repairs made after the wake of the great storm, when a new roof had been put on the dairy, Rafael left them. The country had a newly elected president, Dr. Illia, and there was hope that the economy would improve. Plans to pave the road around the central plaza in Las Rosas went forward, and Rafael got a job with the crew.

"But if ever you need me, Patrón," he told Michael, pushing back his old black felt hat, "you know where I live." And they shook hands.

Diana took his hand also and pressed it hard between both of hers. "Thank you, Rafael. Thank you for everything."

He turned his head shyly away and tried to withdraw his hand, but Diana held on until he was forced to look back into her eyes.

"It's all right," he mumbled, hunching his shoulders.

"I shall miss you."

He smiled then, pulling his hat down low over his forehead, and she let him go.

But before he left, he held out his hand to Philip. "*Chaú*, little one. May God keep you."

They watched him pedal away on his trusty old bicycle until he reached the gate. After that, only the speck of black that was his hat could be seen on the horizon, silently winging its way up to the high road, where it disappeared from sight.

"I shall miss him," Diana said again.

"Yes. He was a good worker. I wish him luck. I really wish him well." Michael turned his gaze from the now empty horizon back to her. "He is one of the best natural construction workers I've ever known. The campo is not for him," he said, and the tone of his voice was so wistful, Diana wondered what he was really thinking.

It was hard finding a replacement for Rafael, even when Michael offered to build a house and lease a piece of land to a man and his family. He grumbled that the people, despite the hard times and unemployment, really didn't want to work.

Diana had to take over the milking chores and had little time for Philip and housework because Michael had all he could handle

go to the doctor, too, but they go to her as well, just to be sure. Just to be safe, you understand."

"I see. Just to be sure."

"Yes. Why not?" Manuel grinned slyly. "One never knows." He winked at her. "It doesn't hurt."

"Does she use herbs and things like that?"

"Oh, no! All she needs to know is your name and where the pain is. She concentrates on it. You don't even have to go yourself. You can send someone else."

"My goodness! How much does she charge?"

"Nothing. She doesn't need money. Her husband makes enough."

"Do you really believe, Manuel, that she can cure you like that? From a distance? Like the farmer who can make worms leave calves—from a distance?"

"Hah! No." He laughed easily. "I don't believe that. But the curandera is different. Everyone goes to her. I have a bad back, you know. And she's helped me many times."

"I see," Diana frowned, settling back against the trunk of the great tree.

"There are many things we can't understand, Señora."

"I know."

"This tree, for instance. Some people believe it has magical powers. Then some say that sorrow and finally ruin come upon the house on whose roof the shadow of the ombú falls. Even birds will not nest in it. Have you never noticed?"

Diana looked up into the mass of large, glossy, deep green leaves above their heads. "Yes.... You're right. Manuel, do you believe in ghosts?"

"Of course. But I am not like my mother. Old people see ghosts everywhere. She is always afraid I might stay too long here after dark."

"Why?"

"Because she believes that is when the souls of the dead are riding about, asking for our prayers. But sometimes doing mischief as well."

"Are there any here?"

"Well, Señora, of course. But I do not believe that the spirit of the poor gaucho who is buried here under this ombú is evil. Though it can be dangerous at night when he decides to go riding around the countryside, leading horsemen astray, confusing them,

"Nothing."

"Yes. And he let him hang there until he rotted, and his flesh fell to the floor. Then he took what was left of him and scattered him out in the field here, in front of the casco, but, of course, it was the gauchos' house then. Their dormitory. And the poor Señorita, she had to watch while the vultures picked his bones clean. They say she laughed, but the truth is that later in the night she collected her lover's bones and buried them here under the ombú. Then she rode away in the dawn and hid out from her father in Buenos Aires with some foreign people. After that, old don Pedro killed himself. In grief, they say. Hung himself from this very tree."

Overhead a carpenter bee was humming loudly, looking like a ball of shining gold among the dark green vegetation that resembled laurel.

When she finally spoke, it was in a whisper, "So...so misfortune did come to that house...."

"Yes, I suppose so, Señora. But that was long ago. Now the people say no one, not even a *ghost*, could live with the noise. Even the walls shake when it's on."

"The generator?"

"Yes! Your generator."

"I know," she smiled.

"Your generator has scared the ghost out of the casco. That's what some people say."

"Yes." She laughed briefly. "Perhaps."

without mercy. The corn began to shrivel up, the sunflowers stopped growing and bent their heads in woe, the pastures turned brown, crackling underfoot like paper, and the wheat ripened before its time.

Michael and Diana tried to save the alfalfa by baling it, getting up at three each morning and working until eleven, by which time the day was so hot the old baling machine they had rented would overheat and refuse to move.

Every dawn was full of fire, but the day ended without fulfilling its promise of rain.

A few days before Christmas Michael announced at breakfast, "Yesterday, when I was at the bank, the manager was predicting disaster as a result of this drought. First time I've seen him so down. He said everyone was to gather today at the church to pray for rain—"

"Perhaps we should go."

"Crazy! What would people think? I've really gone off the deep end? I'm not *that* desperate."

Diana wanted to add, "But I am," though she held her tongue, and only said, "It might be interesting for Philip to see...."

They came upon the procession forming outside the church facing the central plaza in Las Rosas. The priest was dressed in his golden robes, preceded by an altar boy carrying a tall cross and another bearing the chalice, followed by four more altar boys, each carrying one end of a richly decorated platform upon which stood the patron saint of Las Rosas: St. Francis, the guardian of the earth and its creatures, big and small. Behind the priest marched several more altar boys in white gowns, followed by the men of the village who otherwise never went to church. Church was for the women. On Sundays they would escort them to mass, deposit them in the cold, dark cathedral, and then retreat to the warmth and camaraderie of the sidewalk outside. There, dressed in black suits, shiny with wear, they would exchange pleasantries among themselves until the service had come to an end. But now they fell into line behind the priest, while their women stood aside.

Michael watched in silence for a while before, without saying a word, he suddenly left Diana's side and joined the men. Andrews followed him. Then there was Carlos, the Admiral, the manager of the Banco de la Nación himself, as well as the local grain merchant with his shriveled arm. They marched along with the school children from both the public and convent school, together with the

Diana ran outside into the night where the stars were still shining and danced in her bare feet and long white nightdress in the open field before the ombú with Alex barking crazily after her. She was not afraid. Rather she felt that if the gaucho buried there could, he would join her.

Clouds raced back and forth across the heavens covering and then uncovering the persistent stars, like dancers whipped to a frenzy in accompaniment to Diana's movements. Within five minutes of her performance, these clouds succeeded in extinguishing these stars, and the rains came as though a gigantic dam had broken open above her head. Diana fled back to Michael's wondering arms thoroughly drenched.

But the rains were too heavy and had come too late to save the crops.

"You danced too well," Michael kidded her. "Next time, go easy."

He wasn't angry, like she. He didn't demonstrate his disappointment with the harvest, which to her only meant that they would have to wait another year for the baby she needed, for the baby she began to crave more and more urgently with each passing day. "Why," she turned on him soon thereafter, "I even think you're glad!"

"You fool," he told her coldly, without raising his voice, and turned away to ride off on Bucephalus. He returned only after dark. Manuel had long since left, and Diana had had to milk the cows. His supper was waiting for him on the stove and Philip was already in bed when he walked in to find her sitting at the kitchen table, staring down at her empty plate. The eyes she turned to him were red from crying. He took her into his arms.

"You must understand," she murmured, "to live in this land and not be fertile is an abomination."

"Oh, but I do understand." And he took her to bed.

Six weeks later Michael brought her the news. At first, she tried waiting for him by the casco, then under the ombú. Finally, unable to stand the suspense any longer, she and Philip, accompanied by Alex, wandered slowly down the road, picking wildflowers on their way. By the time the truck had made the turn from the high road onto the colony road, Diana had reached the gate and held it open for Michael.

"How's the new little mother?" he called out to her as he drove

And for no reason at all, except that he wanted to lighten her chores, he would sometimes announce: "Darling, I love you."

When all the long day's tasks had been accomplished, and Philip was safely asleep in his bed, Diana sat under the ombú with only Alex, her guitar, and the stars to keep her company. And the sweet satisfaction of feeling a new life stirring within her.

She came to look for the moon, she realized, for the first time in her life and watching for its arrival in the east was almost as pleasurable as waiting for the sun to rise in the same place half a day before.

The moon has a special light on the pampas. In the summer when it is full, it turns the fields white and makes them glow softly in the night, and it lays down a rope of white upon the flat and featureless roads, which stretched there, it would seem, into infinity over the edge of the world. In the autumn it rises early before the sun has gone to shine on the other side of the earth. Then, reflecting the sun's fading glory, it is a huge orange moon that crouches for a long time on the horizon before lifting itself up to begin its journey across the starry sky, turning first yellow, and then white, as it climbs high into its timeless orbit. At that moment, together with all its companion constellations, it sparkles in the heavens like sunlight on water running swiftly in a woodland brook.

Diana enjoyed it most of all when there was a wind, and the moon played hide-and-seek with the white clouds, racing hither and yon but going nowhere in a blue-black sky. At times like these, the ombú would murmur and moan, sometimes even roar with excitement. And Diana liked to lie on her back, cradled within its roots stretching out into the pampa, and looking skyward, rub her belly, grateful for the thousandth time for the life that was growing within her, and all about her.

But the most surprising thing of all, she found, was what a full moon on a quiet night could do to the ombú. Glancing from Philip's window one night around midnight when the moon was directly overhead, the whole tree, from its great roots to its topmost leaves, could be seen from a distance shining like white fire.

One noon she and Philip picnicked under the ombú. When she lay down to rest afterward, she fell asleep with him. In her dreams she heard the sounds of footsteps coming and going, the voices of people talking, the noises of dogs and chickens, and a little girl shouting and laughing. The child was dressed in a white, old-fashioned dress with a ribbon in her hair and one around her hips, sing-

calving rope hanging from the corral fence and followed Rosa in the pickup. When she arrived at their farm, she saw to her disgust that the two brothers were trying to pull the calf out of its mother with their tractor.

Rosa explained that when it wouldn't come they had tried pulling it first with one horse, then with a team of horses, and, finally, in desperation, they had resorted to the tractor.

"It was then I told them to get you," Mrs. Berrato said, plainly distraught as she glared angrily at her two sons. "It's my best cow, and I don't want it to die, as do all the cows when we have to use the tractor on them."

She turned to Diana and raised her two hands together as if in prayer, tears now in her eyes that had long since lost their color along with her worn and wrinkled pale face that looked as though it had never seen the sun. As if she had spent her life in a cellar rather on the sun-drenched pampas surrounding her. "Help me, doña Diana," begged the old woman. *"I know you can."*

Diana told Rosa, "First, take that chain off the calf's hooves." Then she stroked the head of the exhausted, half-dead cow, loosening the lasso around its neck which was holding the animal to a tree so tightly that half of its face was scraped raw from the bark. Diana gave her water all the while talking to her in English, giving courage not only to the cow, but to herself as well, until she was sure the cow's labor efforts had returned. Then, with the aid of her rope tied around the ankle of each tiny hoof, she slowly, carefully, helped the cow to deliver her calf successfully.

Only the old woman thanked her. The rest of the family stood about staring, dumbfounded. "It was luck," Diana assured them. Rosa's sister-in-law smiled weakly, her two little boys clinging wide-eyed to her housedress. Her husband looked back sullenly at Diana after starting up his tractor anew, and took off without a word, leaving the women to care for the newborn calf.

tractor, or horse and wagon was in the procession that stretched for more than a mile, slowly following the ceremonial hearse through the streets of El Trebol and out of town to the cemetery, as the bells in the church tower tolled mournfully. "Who? Who? Who?" they seemed to cry.

The cemetery, like so many others on the pampas, was a square plot of land, lonely and isolated from the town. Surrounded by a high masonry wall, it contained stone and marble monuments to the dead—edifices far more imposing than the homes of the living in the town. The dead were laid in the middle of an open prairie, far away from family, friends, and neighbors, without even a tree to shade them from the summer sun, to shelter them from the wind and rain. Only two tall poplar trees stood guard, like sentries, on either side of the iron grill gate.

Only poplars. Perhaps, Diana observed, because it is the tree which always sighs, as it bends with the wind—no matter from which direction it blows.

As they stood there, not too far from the mausoleum of the Rossio family, the largest in the cemetery, the people around them began to whisper about what had brought them there. The police had said there was no sign of robbery. No witnesses had come forth. No one had even heard the shots. Philip remained unmoving, gripping Diana's hand tightly, staring, uncomprehending, as the coffins were lowered into the ground.

She looked about her at the desolate scene and whispered to Michael, "Promise me you will never bury me in a place like this."

"I understand."

"Under the ombú," she said.

"Under the ombú," he promised.

"And for you?"

"For me?" He thought for a moment. "Scatter my ashes," he whispered, "at the four corners of our land."

She gripped his hand. "I promise."

Michael insisted on visiting the family after the services, telling Diana he must find out as much as he could. "My machine," he looked grimly at the closed factory gates, "is in there."

A man they did not know, a salesman who happened to be passing through El Trebol that day, stood on the edge of the crowd gathered outside the Rossio home waiting to pay their respects. Diana heard him observe, to no one in particular, "It's better they

done this to me? To my family? Does God hate me so?" she demanded.

"Mama...." Lila tried to take her in her arms, but she pushed her away. "Why has He done this to me? *Is there no justice?* I have worked so hard to make this a respectable family! I have followed all the rules!"

She ran to the door, opened it and shouted to the people gathered in the street. *"Is there no justice?"*

Tomás pulled her back into the parlor. "Does He do these things just to keep us like sheep?" she demanded of her husband. "Never knowing when something like this will happen? When the forces of evil are going to strike? In the night? Without warning? Or is this living just a lottery?" his wife begged to know, as she crumbled down next to him on the sofa.

But all Señor Rossio could do was continue to moan, his head in his hands again, "Without Maria, I am lost."

On the way home Diana ventured to ask, "What do you think will happen now? Do you think Rossio will change his mind about the machine?"

"I don't know." Michael attempted to reassure her. "It just might take longer. Until they get everything settled."

It was past midnight by the time they reached their campo, and Philip had long since fallen asleep. But when Diana placed him in his bed, he opened his eyes and asked her, "Darling?"

"Yes?"

"Darling...."

"Yes, my love?"

"When are they...," he hesitated, searching to find the words he needed. "When are they going.... When are they going to let those poor ladies out of their boxes?"

"Ah...." She hugged him. "Their spirits are already gone. To heaven." She pointed to the night sky outside his window. "It's just their bodies that are there."

"Where is heaven?"

Heaven, she wanted to answer, is a place where, once you go there, you can never come back. But instead she answered Philip, "Heaven is where God lives."

"Who is God?" he immediately asked, sitting up now, no longer sleepy.

Diana was taken aback. Perhaps living as close to nature as they

SEÑOR Rossio arrived unexpectedly at the campo in the late afternoon a week after the funeral, accompanied by his daughter Lila. Diana welcomed them. "Michael will be here shortly after he finishes the evening milking. How is everything going at the factory?"

"We've closed down for two weeks out of respect for Maria," he answered and sank down with a sigh onto the couch before the fire, his big, round bowling ball of a bald head bent forward, his hands resting on his knees as he stared into the flames.

"When the police captain told me who had done it, I thought I would faint," he said. "I couldn't believe it."

Lila also appeared exhausted as she sat beside her father. "And I lost my milk," she announced. "Mama and I worked all day trying to get the baby to drink from a bottle, but she just cried and cried. It was horrible. She was so hungry, and she couldn't understand." Lila shook her head, trying to control the tears which came into her eyes. "She still doesn't like the bottle and sometimes cries all night."

"You know?" Diana looked at Rossio's gray face and was all at once afraid of what would be his reply.

"You haven't heard?"

"No."

"I thought everyone knew."

"No one tells us anything. People seem to think we know everything, or should know."

Just then Michael appeared. Rossio waited for him to remove his muddy boots at the door before announcing, "It was Ricardo who killed her. His own aunt. Ricardo, the son of my brother, José."

Michael sat down heavily, as though he had received a blow.

"But why?" Diana asked.

"Because," Lila answered, her voice hard and bitter now, her tears gone. *"Because she always knew he was no good.* And he couldn't stand that."

Rossio began to explain. "He says that she hated him and always favored my son Tomás over him. Which I cannot deny, because she was right. Ricardo was no good. But then, what can you expect with a mother like he has—a common girl from one of those

wasn't his fault at all! That it was Maria's own fault because she didn't like him!"

Diana went into the kitchen to get glasses of burgundy wine to warm everyone. It had been a particularly cold and damp day when the clouds had hung low all afternoon, like puffs of ash-colored smoke produced by a white, burnt-out sky.

When she returned to the living room, Lila was talking to Michael. "The reporters were there from Buenos Aires and Rosario. At first, Tomás got the police captain to agree not to tell them anything. It would only be bad for the town. But they found out anyway and printed it in all the papers. Ahee!" she wailed, "poor Tomás. He is engaged, you know, to a girl from Buenos Aires. An excellent family, and he is afraid they might call it all off now because of this. I don't know how *I* can ever return to school."

"But why not?" Diana asked.

"Because I could never again command authority from the children."

"So everyone knows," Michael said.

"Oh, yes," Lila said. "By late afternoon—the day after the funeral—everyone knew. Many people gathered in front of the police station. They wanted to go in and get him. But when the police captain saw this, he sent for the mayor. You know that Andrews, the Englishman, is our mayor now, don't you?"

"No, I didn't."

"He came all the way in from his estancia to speak to the crowd. It was he who also had to authorize Ricardo's transfer by the Policía Federal to San Jorge, fifty miles north of El Trebol. There he would be safe from the crowd. And I tell you the Policía Federal arrived just in time, too, before the people stormed the police station. Andrews was speaking to them outside in front, trying to assure them justice would be done, while they were taking Ricardo out by the back door."

"And his mother followed him all the way to San Jorge in her car!" Rossio cried out.

"Calm. Papá. Calm," his daughter told him, stroking his arm.

"You know," he said to Michael, still visibly trembling despite his daughter's warning, "the captain told me that the hardest thing he ever had to do in his career was to shake Ricardo's hand at the funeral and offer him his condolences along with all the rest of the family. Maria had been his friend, too. He felt she should be decently buried, without any scandal. And all along he knew who her

"Of course. But it will take a lot of money."

"How can the judge deny the facts?" she persisted.

"Oh, his lawyers will think of something. Probably that he committed a 'crime of passion.' His mother is already going around hinting that she will testify that Maria had been his mistress, and she rejected him."

Although Diana was close to the blazing fire, she shivered.

"But that still doesn't get him off from killing her maid!"

Philip, who had been drawing pictures in his room, came out and stood next to his mother. She put her arm around his shoulders and drew him to her. Señor Rossio smiled at him briefly and took a bag of hard candy from his pocket, but Philip shook his head when Rossio offered it to him. The distraught man did not insist and put the candy on the coffee table in front of the couch.

"No. It doesn't," Rossio acknowledged. "But she was a poor woman, and her family has no money to prosecute."

The room fell silent for a long moment as Rossio stared at the flames in the fireplace as if he had forgotten where he was. Finally, he said to Michael, "My lawyers tell me I should incorporate the company and let them sell out. But this would mean inviting stockholders, having a board of directors who could appoint the company's executives. They could tell *me* what to do, and the company wouldn't be mine anymore. And what would my son Tomás have, I ask you? Maybe nothing in the end."

"What have you decided to do?" Michael spoke quietly, carefully.

"Well, I told those lawyers that I can't do that. I can't do that to Maria, you understand? How could I?" He slumped down onto the couch, and leaned toward the fire, clasping and unclasping his hands. Michael waited.

"José," he finally said, "has agreed not to sell out if I help Ricardo."

"And?"

"What else can I do? Do you realize he could sell to just *any-one*? Someone from the *outside*? Even someone from Buenos Aires who understands nothing?" He glanced helplessly down at Alex, who lay at Michael's feet. In a low voice, muted with humiliation he murmured, "I have agreed to release the necessary funds from the company to pay off the judge."

Diana drew in her breath. She was no longer sorry for him. She was now afraid of him.

"You have no choice, Papá," Lila assured him.

"All that work. He calls it *his* machine now. It's *my* machine, damn it!" He hit the brick wall of the kitchen until his fist bled. Philip knelt down in the doorway and hugged Alex, burying his head in the dog's thick mane.

"His workers could never have done the job!" Michael shouted. "They are very skilled in tooling, yes, but they could never have done the engineering, known how to make the parts, and get the ones they couldn't make."

He left the kitchen and returned to the fireplace, stoking the logs. "How about that?" he asked. "He got a top-notch engineer for nothing, and now he wants my campo as well!"

"Is it true?" Diana quietly asked. "That we are behind at the Banco de la Nación?"

"Yes."

"Why?"

"Interest rates have gone up on our initial government loan. And then there are the payments for our equipment, which must be matched in dollars. Remember we borrowed when the peso was eighty to the dollar. Now it is three-fifty and going up every day, but the dollar amounts we owe remain the same. And inflation has not kept pace with the government-controlled price of milk or meat."

"But I thought we were breaking even."

"Not exactly. I needed money for the prototype of the milking machine."

"*You* paid for it?"

"Of course. I had to. It was our chance. An investment. Don't worry, though. We can make it up. We have enough resources around here."

"Not the cows."

"No," he agreed.

Later that night, however, Michael wondered, "It might just be the answer—"

"Nonsense. And then what would we do?" The thought of losing the campo made her sick. "We will find the money elsewhere. Anyway, with everyone without money, we'd have to sell the pedigree cows just for meat. But even that won't work. We still haven't finished paying for them. What about the heifers? The steers?"

"I'll try," he promised. "I'll try."

She wrapped herself tightly around his body that night. "Can you feel him?" she whispered.

IN the morning the hitching mechanism on the tractor snapped. "Only place I can get one made right away for this Fordson is in Rosario," decided Michael. Before leaving, he added, "I think I might as well stop by San Juan on my way back and talk to the Duchess."

"Good idea! And don't worry about me. I'll be all right," Diana assured him.

At ten o'clock in the evening Alex announced the arrival of a car after Diana had already gone to bed. Quickly wrapping her long, bulky, scarlet woolen robe about her, she went out to see who it was.

Diana had never seen the man before, but he appeared to know who she was. "Tell your husband that I just met your cows on the high road heading for Las Rosas," the stranger called to her without getting down from the cab of his pickup. "Someone must have left your gate open or someone opened it on purpose."

"Don Miguel is not here. Are you sure they are our cows?"

"I don't know. But someone better come and see. Where is your peón?"

"In Las Rosas. I'll come myself. Can you drive me?"

"Sure, Señora, but you'll need a couple of horsemen."

"Don't worry. If they are really mine, I won't." And she hopped up into the truck without daring to take the time to return to the casco to dress.

Surely enough, the stranger was right. As he drove up behind the cows, Diana recognized them in the headlights of the man's car as her own. They were running rapidly along, about fifty of her best milkers, spread out across the road. She remembered releasing them after the evening milking into the pasture near the old gate, but at that time it had been closed. Who had come by since then? she wondered. What was more puzzling was who, if they had done so, had been so irresponsible as to have left it open? Certainly not someone from the area. They would know that once seeing the gate open, the cows could have easily been tempted to demolish the pasture fencing. All it would take was a half-wild leader among them to find a weak point and the others would follow.

"Then it cannot wait." Mopping his brow rapidly with an already soiled large brown handkerchief, sweating although the weather was chilly, he said, "Doña Diana, allow me to present," he turned to the man in the shiny black suit, "Señor Ortega. He is the tax collector of the Province of Santa Fe."

Ortega held out his hand briefly without speaking or returning Diana's smile. The two policemen looked away, standing at attention like soldiers, two big revolvers hanging conspicuously from both sides of the leather belts around their waists.

"As the former director of this colony," Señor Montoya threw back his head, and looking directly into Diana's eyes, announced in a loud and official tone of voice, "I've been asked to inform you and your husband of a judgement that has just been rendered against you by the court of Santa Fe."

"For what?" she asked as her voice almost failed her, glancing at the policemen's revolvers and remembering the warning given her by a friend in the U.S. Embassy before she left for Argentina. "In South America the gringo never wins."

"Back taxes. If you do not immediately pay the three years of back taxes you owe, I will be forced to execute the court's order and evict you from this campo immediately."

The two policemen grinned sardonically as the tax collector, looking like a vulture in his shiny black suit, his eyeballs tinged with yellow, handed Diana the court order. The four men filled the spacious room, and there did not appear to be any air left for Diana to breathe. The walls of the room began to move before her eyes, and the faces of the men blurred, merging together into something diabolical.

"There has been some mistake," she managed to reply, her voice shaking. "When we bought this land the Consejo told us that we did not have to pay taxes for five years. Those are the conditions given to all farmers who buy Consejo land—"

"Yes," answered Montoya, "but those were rules which applied to the *colonias*. When you bought this land it was no longer part of the colony. The colony had been terminated. It was twenty years, if you will recall. Twenty years—the lifetime of the colony."

The ruthless-looking man in black spoke for the first time. "I shall initiate proceedings immediately. I cannot wait. I have my instructions."

"Come, doña Diana," old Montoya said, smiling slyly now. "Why cause all this trouble for yourself? Just give the gentleman

"But there were the policemen! They were armed. I recognized one of them. They were *real*. And the tax collector was serious. Here, read for yourself." She handed him the court order and other documents the tax collector had given her. "He intended to occupy our campo. Yesterday."

"Nonsense! It was a plain old extortion scheme, and you fell for it. Why didn't you tell them you had the money in the bank?"

"Because they knew I had it here! They know we still haven't paid the bank. Oh, what does it matter anyway? If we owe it, we owe it. We can always find money another way."

"For instance?"

"We could take out a second mortgage on the campo."

"I've already tried that. The rates are too high now. *Thirty-three and one-third percent*. With what we have left, we would never be able to meet the payments. And judging from the way things are going around here, they wouldn't hesitate to foreclose at the first opportunity."

"Can't you ask Dragonetti in the Consejo to help us get the money back?"

"Dragonetti is dead. He died soon after we bought the campo. And, anyway, you can never get money *back* from the state. A credit, maybe. But I doubt it."

He left the kitchen and collapsed in the armchair next to the fire, taking the documents with him. He looked them over and eventually acknowledged, "Those papers are real enough, but the thing that bothers me is why now? Is it possible that Rossio wants this land that badly? Manuel said he overheard old Montoya's son boasting at the cheese factory that Rossio would give him a milking machine once he got this land."

"You mean, you think Rossio is behind this tax thing?"

"Probably. He has influence enough."

"Oh, poor sweetheart." She didn't dare tell him about the lost cows, the open gate. Now, she realized, it could have been Montoya's son, or even an agent of Rossio who had done it. She knelt beside him and put her arms around his waist. "The trouble is you showed them too well. Before we came, Montoya would have nothing to do with milking."

"Yes, *sure*. And I wonder what Rossio's next move will be. I should be able to sue him for my machine, but that would be useless, given his connections. Perhaps it would be better to sell to him before it is too late."

the food pass the lump in her throat, feeling at times as though it were strangling her. Only Philip ate well, asking for second helpings. "More, darling, more," he kept saying, trying to please. He seemed so full of life. And his eager gray eyes, sparkling like sunshine on polished silver, laughed at them, urging them to smile back at him.

Precisely at noon and before they had completely finished their lunch the kitchen suddenly darkened. Michael sprang up to see if a storm was on its way across the pampas. He immediately came running back, calling out, "It's an eclipse! A solar eclipse! Quick! Get your sunglasses! Come and see!"

Facing east, they watched as the moon on the far horizon passed between the earth and the sun, like a thief stealing the great star's radiance and warmth. The bright white light of midday turned green. When the sun was completely covered, blotted out, the little light that escaped from around the moon's circumference changed the world to dark blue: the sky, the fields, the trees, Michael's and Philip's faces. Even cinnamon-blond Alex turned blue. Everything became perfectly still. Not a leaf stirred, nor a blade of grass moved.

Alex barked into the void furiously, as he would at an intruder. Then a cold wind began to rustle, ever so slowly at first, in the uppermost branches of the trees, gathering force while the moon gradually moved across the surface of the sun. As it traveled, the dark blue light of midday waxed green again, and the wind picked up speed, chilling them, producing goose bumps on their flesh. Alex stopped barking and cowered behind them.

When the moon had completed its voyage across the face of the sun and daylight was restored, they had no desire to return to their now cold food. Michael went to repair his tractor, and Diana took Philip with her to inspect the calves frolicking in their pasture near the orchard.

~ Part IV ~
Like an Ownerless Horse

Like an ownerless horse the gaucho is,
That everyone may ride.
They break his back and they break his heart,
For life he must struggle from the start,
Like the tree that without a shelter grows
On the wind-swept mountain side…

Martín Fierro, by José Hernández

~

T HE calves gathered about her greedily sucking her fingers, her entire hand, slobbering over her jeans trying to get a piece of its material in their mouths as well. She had a difficult time to keep them from butting her as they would their own mother.

She sensed a storm gathering yet continued to play with the animals until Michael appeared at the edge of the pasture, calling for her to return to the house. As she turned to answer him one of her calves, three months old and the biggest of them all, rammed its head into her pelvis. The force of the blow knocked her to the ground, and she hurt as though her bone had been broken.

Michael half carried her back to the house just as the southwestern horizon began to darken with a cloud as big as a mountain. The pampero that had been defeated in the morning now returned to strike the weakened sun with a vengeance. Soon the darkness covered half the sky, followed by lightning that shattered the heavens as though they were glass. Thunder shook the casco before the full force of the storm struck, roaring in the trees like a dozen express trains passing through.

Michael and Philip clustered around her bed. "It's all right," she assured them rolling from side to side clutching her pelvis in pain, struggling to hold onto their baby.

Then the rains of the pampero arrived, making it impossible for either horse or car to reach Las Rosas and the doctor. The roads would soon become a morass of sticky red clay in which a horse could break its legs, and through which a car, even a truck or jeep, could not get more than fifty feet before its wheels would be packed up to its chassis with the clay.

But when the contractions started, Michael decided to go for help, using the tractor. Diana begged him not to leave her. "I must try," he told her. "I've gotten through in worse storms than this."

She watched him mount the tractor and proceed carefully down the road in the heavy rain. Once past the gate, he zigzagged from one side of the road to the other to keep from getting stuck. When he reached the high road, he disappeared from sight.

He had been gone two hours when she knew the baby was coming. She calmly ordered Philip to leave the room and closed the

her cheeks was pulled taut over her bones and burned as though fueled by the fire that was consuming her womb. Only her lips trembled as she stood, unmoving, behind the bars of the window, watching Michael pray over their son's grave.

Philip and Alex stood silently apart in the open field. Suddenly the silence of the oncoming night was broken by the sound of a horse galloping rapidly across the fields. It was the white stallion returning, coming out of the north, racing across the pastures. He passed close to the ombú before leaping the fence and disappearing into the monte.

"Halfway to Las Rosas," Michael explained, holding her hand, "the tractor wouldn't move anymore. The mud had packed itself like cement by then, and the wheels wouldn't even spin. So I left it and continued on foot. The mud was so bad that by the time I got to the doctor's I was as exhausted as a man who has just traveled through a blizzard. And then I found he wasn't even there."

"It doesn't matter. He couldn't have done anything, anyway."

She slept fitfully, and by morning realized the burning she felt within her was the result of a high fever. By the time the taxi arrived she was in great pain. The road was still impassable except for cars like the Model T, with its small bicycle-like tires and chassis suspended high from the ground. With each bump in the road Diana cringed in agony and dug her fingernails into the upholstery with one hand and clung tightly to Michael's arm with the other to keep from screaming. Philip sat in front with the anxious taxi driver. When they reached Las Rosas, Diana asked him to stop in front of the tailor's house.

The tailor's wife opened the door, and Michael thrust Philip into her arms. "Please take care of him. My wife is very sick, and we must go to the doctor's."

They did not know the young doctor who greeted them in Dr. Hilli's office. He explained that he had arrived that morning to handle any emergencies that might arise during the old doctor's absence.

After examining Diana he became agitated and told Michael that she was too ill to be transported all the way to the hospital in Rosario. The D and C would have to be done immediately to keep the infection from spreading further. However, since it was Sunday, the woman who administered anesthesia in Las Rosas was also away.

"I shall have to proceed without it, Señora," he told her. "Please try to be brave."

Only you and I. There is nothing else," she cried as she tried to hold onto the outer edges of sanity.

"You are wrong," he told her. "There is Philip. You must not reject him."

When Manuel heard what had happened, he arrived on schedule every morning, along with the sunrise. Later in the week he and Michael met in the course of their chores near the orange tree outside Diana's open bedroom window.

"I feel," she heard Michael confess, "as though I am on a carousel called bad luck, and I can't get off. I just keep going around and around. I can't get off."

"I understand," Manuel sighed. "When misfortune has singled out a man for its prey, it will follow him to the end. He will not escape from it though he reach up to the clouds like an eagle, we say, or thrust himself deep into the earth like the hairy armadillo."

"How jolly!" Michael tried to laugh. "You aren't very optimistic people, are you?"

"It is our nature. But I, personally, would say that misfortune is more like a hardy tree. When you cut off one branch, sure enough, it sprouts another. You have to pour poison into its roots to kill it."

"What do you mean?"

"Patrón, get away from this place."

It seemed an interminably long time before Michael answered, "I cannot. Doña Diana would never leave. And, besides, I have nowhere else to go."

"Patrón, that cannot be true. Not a man like you."

After that Diana began to imagine that Michael was thinking of leaving her. She accused him, as she tossed in bed with the fever, of wanting to return to London.

He did not answer her. He could only hold her in his tired arms, stroking her forehead and pushing back her long, sweat-soaked hair, forcing her down onto her pillow where he spread it out around her, like a veil, to dry.

Diana became afraid whenever he left her bedside, even though he assured her time and again he loved her and would not leave her. Once when he held her she caught a glimpse over his shoulder of the gaucho's face in the bathroom mirror, staring at her. It was not angry, nor sinister. It did not smile. It was just *there*. This time she noticed a sweat band encircling his forehead and disappearing into the thick black hair that covered his massive head. She shuddered. "The face," she whispered. Michael turned around. But the face in

back for once, can't I? Don't I have the right?"

"I'll tell them."

"And don't leave me!" she called after him. "Come right back!"

Diana watched and listened from Philip's room as Michael explained to the woman that his wife was much better now and would not need her. He would pay her a week's wages anyway for her trouble and told her to wait in front of the casco for her husband, who was helping Manuel with the milking. He hurried away to talk to him. As they waited, the little girl wandered over to the ombú to play. Her mother, carrying the baby, followed.

Watching this, wave after wave of renewed jealousy coursed through Diana's body. Loathing and revulsion propelled her out of the house and sent her running toward the intruders under the ombú. Wearing only her nightdress, and with her hair flying about her face, her eyes wild with fury and pain, she shrieked at them. "Get out of there! Get away from there! *Please*," she screamed. "Get away!"

The frightened young woman backed away, stumbling over the roots and the grave of Diana's son. Holding onto her little girl's hand, she ran as quickly as she could toward the dairy with her baby in her arms.

After they had gone Diana tried to explain to Michael, "I could not have had them here, you understand that, don't you darling?"

"Yes, of course."

Diana did not believe him.

"It's the fever," he assured her.

"Oh, I'm so sorry." She began to sob again, burying her face in her pillow.

"It's all right," he said stroking her hair. "It's all right. You will get better, you will see. I shall take care of you myself. I shall sit right here next to you as long as you like."

"All day?"

"All day and all night."

"Promise?" she asked, reaching out for his hand.

"I promise. Manuel can handle everything. What doesn't get done, doesn't get done."

"I wonder how she ever agreed to come here in the first place? No one else ever would."

"She is a practical woman. Her husband has been out of work for months."

"She probably thinks I am crazy and is telling all kinds of sto-

to the airport kept losing his way. After a while, I realized he was doing it on purpose. He didn't want me to leave, and I almost didn't make it."

"He was in love with you?"

"Yes."

"It was Lechien, wasn't it?"

"Yes.

"Well, I don't blame him. Who could not help being in love with you," he murmured, pushing back her hair with one hand and gently caressing the outline of her face, throat, and breasts with the other. Under his touch she felt beautiful once again.

"Oh, was I ever exhausted that night," she remembered.

"You fell asleep almost immediately."

"I know and I shall never forget how shocked I was to wake up in your arms, with you smiling down on me. How did you ever dare do that? To a perfect stranger?"

"It was you. You who did it. You snuggled so beautifully against me after you dozed off. What else could I do but make you comfortable? Holding your head in my lap, I watched you. I had the privilege of looking at your face all the way to Cairo."

"It was so strange," recalled Diana. "The plane was dark. I didn't even know it was you I had sat down next to. I had never done that before. Just go off to sleep. Boom! Like that. Without even looking to see who was sitting next to me."

It was six A.M. when their plane landed in Cairo, and a limousine was waiting for Michael. He offered to take Diana to her hotel. At noon a bouquet of red roses arrived at her door. So many roses she didn't even count. When they met for dinner, he carried more roses in his arms.

He had planned to stay only two days in Cairo, visiting the new Portland Cement factory his company had built. However, he stayed on, showing her the city, the bazaars, the museums, the Pyramids.

"I shall always remember the Cairo museum," she told him. "How dark and gloomy it was, stuffed with treasure, all thrown together without any order, or information. Mummy after mummy after mummy. Stacks of them, almost no guards at all."

"It was a great place for lovers."

"Ah, Cairo! Crazy, beautiful Cairo. Will you take me back there someday? Just for a visit? I would like to see Cairo with you once again."

"Of course," he promised. "We'll go back. Some day."

"He taught me everything I knew," she cried, all the while attempting to steady herself in front of Michael. "He was brilliant, yet the kindest, most gentle of men. He was like a father to me."

"I understand."

Then she turned abruptly away and ran into the monte to hide. Michael did not follow.

But she didn't find peace there. Gone was the sense of enchantment Diana had become accustomed to feeling within the depths of her forest.

The new owner of the white stallion knew it had returned to the monte but never came back to collect him. The mare had also escaped from the glue factory and was wandering around the countryside, no one knew where, while her mate waited for her to find her way home again. He appeared never to rest, day or night, keeping close to the fence, traveling the entire perimeter of the monte over and over, searching for her out on the pampas that encircled his home like the sea.

Diana's unexpected sense of loss over Lechien's death only added fuel to the fire of her nightly melancholy. Sometimes she was sure she was going mad. Yet, with the coming of dawn, she felt perfectly sane. So great was the difference between her feelings during the day and her longing at night, it made her wonder if she wasn't a split personality. Soon she began to fear that the day person, the sane one, was slowly disappearing and the person of the night was growing in stature. It became increasingly difficult for her to distinguish between reality and her dreams. She tried to fight it and keep up appearances, continuing to go about her daily routine as though she were not under the influence of an almost impossible pain.

Many times Diana had to stifle her urge to scream as she struggled for relief from the mysterious illness that was devouring her. This urge came at the most unexpected times, whether delivering the milk to the cheese factory, shopping in Las Rosas, or feeding the calves. Surely, she told herself, I cannot be like this just because of the loss of my baby. Many women lose babies, and they don't go mad. Or by the death of George. I have not seen or heard from him in eight years.

She felt even worse when Michael had to be away, either at San Juan or running errands in Rosario. Then she had little control, and sometimes screamed out loud, frightening Philip and sending Alex racing to her side. She thought of Lucía, and how she had cried while singing the songs of the pampas during her exile in

Paris. Now tears came to Diana as she sang the songs of her own country. At night she took the guitar out under the ombú and played songs for Philip like "Oh! Susanna," "Old Folks at Home," or "My Old Kentucky Home."

One day in the middle of winter Andrews came to tell them that Ricardo Rossio was back. He had been acquitted of his aunt's murder, and was given six months for killing Gina, but had gotten out in three.

While she was preparing lunch for everyone, she heard the "Star Spangled Banner" on the living room radio. Realizing it was the Fourth of July, she ran from the kitchen and stood in the middle of the room, transfixed, feeling as though she were hanging in midair on the back of a horse in the act of jumping a high fence but who kept on sailing through the air, unable to return to solid ground.

The men watched, puzzled. When the anthem was over, she apologized. "I'm sorry. But it's my song, you see. Today is the Fourth of July. I had forgotten."

"Oh, yes! But of course." Andrews exclaimed, recovering himself. "Let me congratulate you. Your Independence Day."

"It was always hot. The hottest day of the year. Not miserably cold like now," she mumbled, throwing a few more logs on the fire. "And we always cooked hot dogs outside. Roasted marshmallows. There were games and races in the park. Fireworks at night."

Michael studied her carefully, and said nothing.

The faces of the people on the streets of Las Rosas began to resemble people she had known in New York. She would come to a standstill, unable to move, her eyes following the person she thought she recognized until he or she was out of sight. Although these illusions came as a shock at first, she soon became used to them, even enjoyed them. It became a game for her to make the proper connection, to link up the right face with the right memory. Though she called people she met by their real names, she was actually seeing old acquaintances.

Sometimes she thought it was Melvin, the boy she had admired in high school, or George, her leading man in the senior play. On these occasions she would smile and greet the startled strangers with *"Buenos días,"* as though they were old friends before continuing on down the street.

Once she was sure she saw Richard, the boy down the block

etables before you leave. I know you haven't time to grow them yourself anymore."

After they had done so, and as she closed the door of the pickup, Marlena looked into Diana's eyes. "Just try not to let it get you during the day," she warned.

But it already has! Diana wanted to cry out. *It already has.*

One night in the spring she awoke from her dreams certain that someone was calling her. Perhaps it is Philip, she thought, getting out of bed. Michael was sleeping soundly. By the time she reached Philip, who was also sleeping soundly, she realized the call had come from outside the casco. When she opened the front door, she faced a thick wall of fog, higher than the treetops. Hidden from view, a full moon was shining down on it, turning the night into a mass of impenetrable cotton batting. She wanted to ride through its soft, downy whiteness and keep on riding forever and ever.

She saddled Mora, who had been waiting nearby for Michael and the dawn, and, clad only in her nightdress, rode out into total silence. It was as though the fog had put a gag on the world, preventing any sound at all escaping from the earth, even the sounds of Mora's passage upon it. It was like being in that little soundproof room where Philip's hearing had been tested and where you couldn't hear the echo of your own words.

Although she could see absolutely nothing around her, Diana was not afraid. Rather she felt a certain sense of sweet exhilaration as she forced the frightened Mora on from pasture to pasture.

Instinctively, Mora brought her to the herd. Though she couldn't see them, she knew her cows were all around her because a familiar muffled sound drifted up through the fog. She reined in Mora and held her still. What she heard was the gentle, coaxing call a cow murmurs to her newborn calf, encouraging it to find her milk. Although she couldn't see the cow or the calf, she knew the mother had to be the once-wild Bessie. She had become her favorite and best producer, and the sounds of her song to her newborn were sweet to Diana's ear knowing the birth had gone well without her assistance, and the calf was healthy and on its feet.

Only then did Diana remember where she was and urged Mora to take her home, but the horse, for the first time, lost her way. The ghostly effect of moonlight on the dense fog confused her. She tried to follow the fencing which divided the pastures. Up and down the fields she went, with Diana not knowing if she was going toward the casco or away from it. A few times the horse almost ran directly

DIANA struggled through the spring like an automaton, accomplishing her tasks perfunctorily. She could not even find the energy to fill the casco with wildflowers as she was wont to do or with the sprigs of delicate yellow, exotic-smelling mimosa blossoms from the tree on the front lawn when it came into bloom. Michael was especially fond of this tree, recalling that a bouquet of these blossoms, like myriad puffs of downy buttercups, was the favored gift of a suitor to his beloved one in the south of France. The announcement of spring and harbinger of exciting days of ardor to come. Nor did she bother to pick the rosy blossoms of her single pomegranate tree outside the window of Michael's study. Not knowing what to do with a pomegranate, she had preferred to celebrate its flower rather than its fruit, much to the dismay of her Italian neighbors who, before her arrival, had been accustomed to raiding the old orchard for nothing else but this revered fruit.

With the arrival of the summer of 1965, December proved to be especially hot and they were forced out of their tin roof dining-living room to eat Christmas dinner under the willow where the shade was deepest and a little breeze blessedly stirred in its old limbs. Diana sacrificed one of her turkeys that lived in the monte for the occasion, and the bird did not disappoint her. Philip received his first tricycle and tried valiantly to ride it through the grass and down the dry, rutted road leading to the old gate. A new toy called Lego unexpectedly arrived from her mother. It was the first Christmas she had sent him a present and the set of plastic building blocks fascinated him.

Carlos Bauer came to visit Diana one afternoon in May when Michael was at San Juan. She was on her way to get Mora, struggling in her heavy, high rubber boots through a field of sorghum *de elepo*, rye grass, and alfalfa, still wet from a morning shower. Though winter, Michael's pastures were green and the grass tall. As she approached Mora, she looked up and saw Carlos, not far from the gate. He was standing there, his chin nestling in one hand, leaning against a fence post, watching her. How, she wondered, had she not heard his Jeep? She was startled to realize she had been so lost

military coup. A dictatorship."

As she spoke she noticed that Mora was approaching them, discreetly munching on sorghum. She was trying to be as nonchalant about it as possible. Diana saw her chance and quickly put the bit she was holding into Mora's mouth before she could escape.

"And you?" she called out to him. "Do you have a Swiss bank account too?"

"Naturally."

She started to lead Mora toward the corral. "What are you doing?"

"I'm going to saddle her."

"For what? Why don't you ride her like that?"

Diana blushed. Riding bareback was something she had never done before. She had longed to try many times, watching with envy how Manuel and other gauchos could leap up and slip weightlessly across the broad backs of their horses when they were in a hurry. Even Rosa Berrato could do it, though she weighed close to two hundred pounds.

"I never have."

"I'll help you," he told her, slipping through the fence. He showed her how to grab hold of Mora's mane, and then, while she swung one leg over the mare's back, he supported her other leg with one hand, pushing her buttocks up with the broad palm of his other hand until she was seated. They both laughed at her clumsiness, and he laughed at her embarrassment. "In the beginning you can mount her next to a fence until you've learned how to get up by yourself."

The astonished horse, saddle-less, bolted off in the direction of the cows, and Diana waved timidly back at Carlos. Then, gaining confidence, she showed off for him by yelling out as Manuel often did, "*Vaca! Vaca! V a c a a a a!*"

Mora responded splendidly. It was an exhilarating ride at first but became a painful one as Mora, more and more excited with the novelty of so little weight on her back, threw herself into the roundup as though she were young again and back on the polo fields. Diana felt her buttocks crash down harder and harder upon old Mora's back until she thought they were being rubbed raw of jeans, underpants, and flesh as well. By the time she had the herd together in the corral, she slid down from the mare feeling as if she had no bottom left, certain that her jeans were covered with blood.

Carlos was waiting for her. "Are you all right?"

"That one standing behind the little one," she continued, "which we call 'Chicateen,' is 'The Beef' because she is so big and ugly. 'Linda' is a real beauty, and that one standing off by herself is a neurotic loner. She's known as 'La Mala.' Of course, I just drew a blank with a few cows. Some have no distinction at all. One is simply called '96' because that was the number on the ear tag she wore when she arrived. Now this one coming in is a splendid example of a Holando Argentino. I call her 'Star of India' because of the white diamond mark on her forehead. She is from one of your bulls."

Carlos inspected the cow carefully. "She *is* a beauty." Then: "When do you expect Michael?"

"Probably not until tomorrow. He went to San Juan today and generally stays to dinner and sometimes overnight."

"Overnight?" Carlos chuckled.

"Yes. Depending upon the weather. He's helping the Duchess install the same machine as we have. Didn't you know?"

"I guess I've heard something like that."

"We need the money."

"Well, I have to warn you, in case you don't already know, the Duchess doesn't pay. With money, that is."

"What do you mean?"

Carlos hesitated. "Oh," he answered rather vaguely, "she believes that the honor of being associated with a Duchess is payment enough, I suppose."

Diana shook her head. "Hah! I don't think Michael would ever be that silly. Besides, he doesn't even like her. She's awful, you know. Such a hard woman."

"I know. How well I know. She stayed at our place for two weeks when she was looking for an estancia to buy in the area. Treated Marlena like her servant and never even gave her so much as a box of chocolates when she left. She hasn't always been a Duchess, you know."

Diana looked at him, puzzled.

"No. She only married the Duke after the War when he was ruined. For the title, of course. She comes from a very wealthy industrialist family in Holland, but also very common, who has supplied all the money for her new empire. That family of hers taught her how to drive a hard bargain."

By the time Diana had finished milking the cows, the sun had already set, leaving behind a thin trail of purple smoke across the

you see?" she insisted, her voice rising, excited now that she could tell someone other than Michael how she felt. "He's the only one who's ever done anything for the majority, the real people of this country. And you know it, too. You—people like you—just don't want to see the truth. But don't worry," she assured him. "I'm the only one who feels this way. Michael," she lied, "thinks as you do."

She knew that to have even mentioned the name of Perón to a great estanciero like Carlos was a breach of etiquette, at the very least. But she didn't care anymore. Instead of criticizing her though, he looked concerned for her for a long moment, saying nothing.

"You might be right, little one," he finally said, "but it would take many, many years before the old oligarchy lets go. And when they do, I can only hope the Peronistas realize where their real riches lie. It is the land, not industry, which will save them."

"Yes. If they too abandon the farmer as he is abandoned now, all the small farmers like me—not like you—but like Michael and me, they will lose in the end."

Carlos laughed. "They don't care about the small farmer. That is not where the votes are."

"Well, then, let them fail. Someone once said 'people get the governments they deserve.'"

"That's good. Very good. But I wouldn't worry. We have our people, our agents, well placed."

"Where?"

"Everywhere. In the military. Industry. The banks. We don't intend to let this country fall apart. We've put too much into it. Paid too high a price. We exiles have to save it for our children if nothing else." He rose from his chair and leaned his elbow on the mantel. "But aren't you hungry?" He looked at Philip who was stuffing a piece of bread and some cheese into his mouth. "Couldn't you give an old friend and his helper some supper?" he asked, tousling Philip's curls. The boy looked up, smiling affectionately at him.

"Of course. But won't Marlena be expecting you?"

"No. Not at this time. I was supposed to have gone on to El Trebol from Santa Clara."

"You are a little lost then, aren't you?"

"Perhaps," he smiled, "but when I passed your monte, I decided you needed me more." He reached out and laid his hand on her shoulder. "I thought, perhaps, I could cheer you up. My father was a clown, after all."

She laughed but, strangely enough, he did not laugh in return.

pero broke the heads of the sunflowers."

"There is one thing, though," he replied. "You have never to worry about pasture. You have the best in the entire country. I've never seen such alfalfa at this time of year, and the clover Michael introduced has done beautifully,"

"Yes. The milk keeps us going. That's all."

"And you are lucky at that. Most dairies this size have gone bankrupt in these times. But then they don't know how to raise cows as you do. You are incredible, you know."

His eyes looked at her so kindly she wanted to cry. Oh, why, Michael, she silently raged, do you have to leave me alone so much?

"Well, I guess we can hold on," she told him. "In fact, we would be all right if we didn't have cows still to pay for."

"Don't worry. The Southern Cross can afford it."

"It's not that." She turned away, deeply embarrassed.

He took her hands and pulled her gently towards him.

"I didn't mean—"

"I know," he answered. She went willingly into his arms, placing her head against his broad, hard chest with a surrendering sigh. He gently kissed her forehead, and her hair, while she listened to his heart beating against her ear.

"Marlena will worry," she whispered.

"Poor Marlena," he answered, and went on gently caressing her. She had no will to resist because in his arms she all at once felt like a sick child who has returned home and was being comforted. Her defenses tumbled. The wall she had thrown up to protect herself from her loneliness crumbled as though the earth itself had opened up and quickly swallowed every last stone.

"You don't know how many times," he whispered, "I have passed your monte, knowing you were alone, and how hard it was for me not to make that turn into your road. How hard it was to keep on going. But this afternoon I turned before I really knew what I was doing. I don't know why.... I really don't know how I could have done it. But then, you see, I have always loved you. From the very first time I saw you in the post office. You are what I have been looking for. What I should have married. But when I couldn't find you, I thought you didn't exist."

Despite her surrender, a part of her still found the strength to protest. "Marlena loves you."

"I know. But *I* love *you*."

She thought how she and Michael rarely spoke anymore. And

supposed to be. She had made love to a Nazi. Worse: a Nazi who was Michael's best friend. She wanted to run away and hide. Far, far away.

Michael arrived for the morning milking.

"What's the matter with you? You look like you've seen your ghost again."

"There's been another revolution," she blurted out, unable to think of any other reply.

"How do you know?"

"Carlos told me."

"When?"

"Last night."

"Was he alone?"

"Why, yes. He stopped by for a bit to give us the news. Wasn't that nice of him?"

"No."

"Why not?"

"Because he's in love with you, that's why. Any fool can see that. He knew I wouldn't be here. I told him so yesterday morning."

"Oh, darling!" She started to shake. "What is happening to us? I love you. Please try to understand. Tell me you understand. Please believe how much I love you."

"I believe you," he answered sternly, his voice grim. And rode off on Mora to herd the cows. Diana began to cry.

In the evening after Philip had gone to sleep, Diana faced Michael. "He's six now. He will soon be able to start first grade. Don't you think it's time he had his surgery?"

"So you want to leave me? Is that it?"

"No!"

"But I understand. Trust me. I do understand. You are right. And we cannot keep putting this surgery off." He was not angry. "It will be good for you to go back to your country after all this time. And it will be good for Philip to meet his grandmother."

"I don't know about that."

"What do you mean?"

"She's not an easy woman. She and I have never gotten along, especially after my father died. I don't think she even likes me. And she thinks Philip's problem is somehow our fault."

"Your own mother?"

"Yes. My own mother."

T HE next day Diana went alone to the café near the bus stop in Las Rosas, sat down at a table by herself and ordered a cognac. She had seen Carlos' Jeep in town and knew he was in the habit of stopping by the café before returning to the Southern Cross.

She was the only woman present, but she ignored the stares of the curious men at the bar slowly sipping their own cognacs. She kept her eyes on the street, watching for Carlos. Eventually an old gaucho, someone she had never seen before, came over to her table. "*Por favor?* Señora?" he asked, grinning through broken teeth. His face was brown and wrinkled, worn like old saddle leather. The years he had spent on the pampas were etched upon it as though by an artisan, skilled in his craft. Diana nodded, so he picked up his cognac from the bar and returned to sit across from her. "You are waiting for someone? You are lonely?"

"No. I am just resting."

"Ah, yes," he sighed, his tired, dark eyes watering. He withdrew a fine white linen handkerchief from the pocket of his bombachas and wiped them dry.

"These are hard times," he told Diana. "I know, Señora, I know. I myself am just passing through on my way south. To Patagonia where a man can still be free. But I used to be from these parts many years ago. You see, I am one of those few left who can still remember, Señora."

"Really?" Diana was interested. "Remember what?"

He leaned forward. "When thousands of wild horses, giant ostriches, and cattle without end roamed the pampas around here. You know what it means, *pampa*, don't you?"

"No."

"Space. It is the word for space in the Quechua language. The Indians who used to live here. And roam free. The only law we knew then was the law of the facón." He caressed the dagger hanging from his belt. "Now the only law they give to us, to people like me, is the short end of the horn." He laughed, but not with humor.

"Did you ever work at Estancia La Argentina? Did you know don Pedro de Casilda?"

was known only as *el Francés*. The Frenchman. I was there the day he buried her. The day the big house burned down."

"What happened?"

"What happened? Ah, who could ever forget? It happened on Christmas Eve. After we had laid her to rest in the ground. And it happened just as we were leaving the cemetery. We saw a faint glow, like the dawn, on the western horizon. At first, we couldn't imagine what it was. Who could be burning their fields, then, at that time? And at night! It was the foreman who was the first to realize what it was, and all the men galloped off to the monte. But it was too late, Señora. There was nothing we could do. The great house had already burned to the ground by the time we reached it.

"How I felt sorry for that poor man! He was so broken with sorrow that he couldn't even ride with us. Many say he blamed himself for Lucía's death. He just stayed behind in this café, frozen into one position all night, looking toward the west. At dawn, when we returned to tell him there was nothing left, he didn't even ask how or why. He just got up from his chair, walked down the street, turned the corner, and crossed over to the railroad station. He took the first train out and never returned. Some say if he had only stayed long enough to light a candle...."

Diana lifted her glass to her lips. Her hand trembled. Then she saw Carlos enter the café. Their eyes met, and he walked casually over to her table, unable to conceal a boyish grin of pleasure that lit up his face as though a lamp had suddenly been switched on in his head.

The old gaucho muttered, *"Buen días,"* and picking up his glass, sauntered back to the bar.

"I just wanted to tell you I am leaving," Diana said. "I'm going back to New York."

He stared at her. His delight at seeing her vanished.

"It's time Philip had his surgery. Before he enters school, which will be soon."

"There are plastic surgeons here, you know."

"Yes. But none that have ever done the type of operation he needs. They've *seen* it done but have never done it themselves. I should get him the best. Carlos, I want to go back. I need to go back."

"You are right." He took a deep breath. "Can you manage it?"

"Michael is seeing the bank about the tickets. After that, I'll be all right. I have my family, you know."

ing? Or a warning? "Do you think I look like her?"

"*Not at all.*"

Diana discovered that leaving Argentina was not a simple matter of having a ticket and a passport. As residents of the country she and Philip needed exit permits and certificates of good conduct, which she had to get from the police. In addition, Michael had to travel to Rosario to find a notary authorized to sign papers stating that his wife was taking his son out of the country with his consent.

By the time Michael drove Diana and Philip to Cañada de Gomez, where they would take the train to Buenos Aires, he was happy for her. "You should have gone a long time ago."

"Perhaps. But how could I? You will take good care of my campo, won't you?"

"Of course, silly one!"

As they neared the town around noon, a pampero rolled out of the southwest. Black clouds came tumbling over the land towards them, running after them. Michael speeded up, hoping to reach the train before the storm did. They arrived at the station just as the black wall was closing in. The train from Córdoba arrived early. It, too, had been racing to keep ahead of the storm.

Since they were the only ones on the platform, the engineer didn't come to a full stop. He slowed down just long enough for Michael to throw Diana's suitcase up to the waiting conductor. The conductor also grabbed Philip as Diana scrambled aboard. She didn't even have a chance to kiss Michael good-bye. He looked so alone, standing on the empty platform, trying to smile up at her. Though it was high noon, the sky was dark and she worried about his having to head back into the eye of the storm, while she was running away.

As the train gathered speed, Michael ran alongside for as long as he could. "Don't forget to come back!" he shouted.

"I won't!" she answered through the closed window, hoping he could read her lips. "I won't!"

Then she was alone. She felt as though she had been cut in half. She had lived with him, worked by his side for so many years, doing everything together, going through heaven and hell together.... She pulled a notebook from her voluminous handbag and labeled it *New York Diary*. On the first page she wrote, "I am scared. Scared. Scared."

Outside, the ominous black clouds rolled along the horizon on

The loudspeaker announced their imminent departure. They were already one hour behind schedule. But Diana was shocked. Catching sight of the pilot and co-pilot, she approached them.

"You are not going to take off in *that*." She pointed to the storm raging on the other side of the plate-glass windows. "Not in a pampero."

"Of course." The young, handsome pilot from New York laughed, appearing mildly surprised. "We can take off in any weather."

"*Not* in a pampero," she warned him.

"Why not?" the co-pilot asked. "It's just a little thunderstorm."

Their confident grins made her feel foolish. Nevertheless, she told them, "You don't know what you are talking about."

But the gate door to the airfield did not open as announced. The nervous passengers stood in line while the crew drank coffee in the single café still open in the half-deserted terminal.

After fifteen minutes there was a sudden lull in the storm. The wind lay down to rest, the rain stopped, the clouds moved off, and for a moment a sliver of moon could be seen. The pilot quickly put down his coffee, the gate was flung open, and the passengers dashed to the plane. Diana buckled Philip securely into his seat. Before sitting down herself, she glanced at the man behind, who was staring at her, frightened. "It's not over yet, is it?" she asked.

He grinned idiotically. "Oh, these people know what they are doing," he replied without any conviction at all.

She laughed back at him. "Sure."

The plane waded slowly down the flooded runway. Diana felt like screaming, Hurry up! You stupid New Yorkers, don't you realize the pampero is only pausing for breath? She knew that in a few minutes it could turn around to devour them like the great monster it was.

As though heeding her warning, the plane suddenly took off, climbing straight up from the land like a giant arrow shot into the night sky. As it did so, the pampero indeed turned around and caught them by the tail. The wings trembled, then shook violently. The wind tossed the great bird from side to side. Then the storm paused to catch its breath anew. The plane appeared to come to a halt; to hang motionless for a moment in the darkness. The pilot saw his chance. With a tremendous surge of power, he forced his plane higher and higher to soar above the tumult and escape the storm's clutches.

A T first the streets, the buildings, the smells and the sounds, the people of New York City were suddenly so familiar Diana found it hard to believe she had ever been away.

Yet it had changed. The New York that she remembered was a great, sprawling city, throbbing with excitement and vitality. Now she saw it as nothing more than a concrete and glass island, teeming with people who looked neither right nor left at their neighbor. After the silence of the pampa, the city roared with sounds that assaulted her hearing but which seemed to fascinate Philip.

As they sped through neat little towns on the train to Watch Hill, Diana couldn't stop thinking: Small. How small. So hemmed in. How different from her pampa where one goes out and meets the sky and nothing more.

Barbara was at the station to meet them. She had come up from Washington to see the older sister she hadn't seen in so long. She had written, "I think I had better be there with you and mother, in the beginning, at least. Just for a few days, anyway."

When she saw Diana, she greeted her with, "Wow! You look great! What a tan! I've told all my friends about you, and they are very impressed. Imagine having a sister who ropes cattle and all that."

"I don't rope them," Diana laughed. "I just sneak up on them. Talk to them. Trick them because, the truth is, I don't know how to throw a lasso. And they know it, too. How's mother?"

"All right. But she stays in bed a lot. Now, please Diana, don't argue. Okay? That's why I came up. It won't do any good anymore. It's no use. I think it will be all right if you just try to humor her. I think she's really anxious to see Philip, though she won't admit it."

She bent down to give Philip a kiss. "He's lovely," she said. "What beautiful eyes! What beautiful eyes!"

"*Buenos días,*" Philip politely replied.

"Does he speak English?"

"Of course. But only with his father and me. It's Spanish with everyone else. I guess he'll soon get used to the fact that here he can speak English with everybody. I hope!"

Diana's mother was upstairs when they entered the house of her

then she had met Michael and hadn't returned since. Her mother even produced a bottle of wine.

The following morning Diana announced she was going into town to get a pack of cigarettes. She didn't really know where she was going. All she knew was that she had to take a walk.

"Why don't you take the car?" her mother asked.

"No, thank you. I'd rather walk."

"But it's too far!"

"Mother, I do a lot of walking where I live."

"All right." She shook her head. "If you insist. But leave Philip here. I'll take care of him. It's too far for him."

Diana laughed. "He walks more than I do."

She walked slowly at first down the chestnut-shaded streets. Each house was exactly as it had been in her dreams. Except there were no old women rocking on the porches, waiting for her to pass and say, Hello. Perhaps they had all died. She stopped in front of her school. It was closed for a holiday, and appeared exactly as it always appeared in her dreams: deserted. She hesitated briefly before turning into the driveway, feeling like a trespasser. The solid brick building was still beautiful, though small, like everything else. There was graffiti scrawled on the white stone foundation. Despite this, she was satisfied. It was still there.

In the downtown district Diana was stunned to see that the stores were still there, too. Except they didn't look real, either. Many of them were closed. A new shopping center had gone up outside of town. Because she needed to reassure herself she was not dreaming, she reached out and touched the buildings and hoped no one would notice. She stopped and stared for a long time into the windows of what was once Woolworth's. A few flies were caught in a spider's web hanging from the arm of a battered, naked dummy.

She heard someone shout, "Hello there!"

Startled from her reverie, she turned to see that it was the policeman across the street. He had been watching her.

"Hello, there!" he called again and came striding rapidly towards her. "Diana! It's been a long time. Where are you living now?"

"Argentina."

"Where's that?"

"It's a country in South America," she told him, struggling to remember who he was.

"Why would you want to do that? What are you doing down there?"

that. He didn't speak before he was almost four years old. When he finally began, 'darling' was his first word. Besides, 'mother' or 'mommy' are English words and are not spoken in Argentina."

"As you wish, but in this country things are not done like that."

Before going to sleep that night Philip asked, "Darling, where does the electricity come from?" he begged to know. "Where is the generator? I can't find it."

"Not too far from here. But it's a huge one. Not like the little one we have. It's so big it can supply electricity for thousands of homes. And factories as well."

"Can I see it?"

"I'll try to arrange it. I'll ask Grandma."

After kissing him good night and closing his door, she found her mother waiting for her in the hall. "Doesn't he say his prayers?" she asked.

"No...."

"Why not?"

"I don't know.... I guess I never felt any need to teach him. He is with God, you see, all day long on the pampas."

"That is no excuse."

Her mother was sincerely perplexed with Philip. And with her. For one thing, Diana now spoke with a British accent. "I married an Englishman, mother," she explained. "Remember? I've been living with an Englishman for eight years. All the people I know who speak English have been educated in England. The only English I hear on the radio comes from the BBC. I haven't heard an American accent since I left the States."

"Still," her mother replied, "I don't see how you could have forgotten your own native language. Your own mother tongue. People are going to think it's very strange." Then she abruptly announced with a scornful grin, "By the way, George Lechien died."

"I know," Diana quickly retorted, without flinching.

"Oh." The sardonic smile evaporated from her mother's lips.

"Philip wants to know where the electricity comes from."

"Well, then," her mother paused for a moment before deciding, "we shall have to take him to visit the Con Edison plant. I've heard they give tours. I know someone who works there. I'll call him tomorrow and see what we can arrange."

Diana welcomed the opportunity to drive to the plant with Barbara by her side, and Philip in the back with his grandmother. But a

He always hoped Diana was having a good time, and that Philip's visits to different plastic surgeons in New York were proving worthwhile. He never asked when she was coming back. Yet each letter, between every line, he begged her to return to him as quickly as possible. *"Even the ombú misses you, my darling,"* he wrote. *"Once at night I imagined I heard the sound of a guitar coming from somewhere far up among the branches, and it was like a lonely soul crying out in pain."*

Diana told him of her visit to the world-renowned plastic surgeon who had been recommended by Philip's surgeon in England. "We saw Dr. Wolf," she wrote. "He is Director of the Cleft Palate Institute of the new Albert Einstein Hospital. Philip took one look at him, stuffed his entire fist in his mouth, howled in terror, and ran screaming down the hall. It was awful. Though not a word had been said in front of him about what Wolf planned to do, he sensed immediately that this man was going to hurt him.

"Wolf was shocked with the extent of Philip's problem. He has never seen such a complicated case. Although he didn't say so, I think he feels more should have been done for Philip up till now. That the surgeon in England didn't do a good job. He thinks Philip will need several operations over the next three years. God!"

Then Diana took Philip to see another plastic surgeon: Dr. Roberts, who was the head of the Institute of Reconstructive Plastic Surgery at the NYU Medical Center, and the one recommended by Andrews' friend in Buenos Aires. Their first visit took place in the doctor's plush Park Avenue office, which did not frighten Philip as had the Einstein Hospital. The waiting room was filled with elegantly dressed women waiting for, or recovering from, expensive face lifts and nose jobs.

A handsome man, wearing a superbly tailored business suit, the doctor looked kindly at Philip. "This boy has suffered a great deal," he told Diana.

"Yes. I know. But why do you say that? How can you tell?"

"How can I tell? A doctor can look at a patient's eyes," he smiled into Diana's, "and know who he is." Turning to Philip, "At his mouth and tell how he has lived. Especially in my business."

Philip let the doctor examine him. He then told Diana that he could do the surgery in three stages, all within a month. First, he would release the flattened-out nose and build up the underneath portion to give it structure. To provide him with an upper lip, he

"I milk cows."

He laughed. Then she told him about Philip.

He was silent for several minutes before telling her as would a judge coming to a difficult decision: "Philip's problem," he said, "is not just a physical one, but a psychological one as well. There are children born with far worse problems than he. Internal ones. Half hearts and other things of which they will surely die. They have beautiful faces and mothers, family, dote on them. But someone like your son...." He glanced away, turning on his comfortable chair toward a brocade-covered window that looked out on nowhere, silent, thinking. After a minute, he turned back to face her.

"He has a problem that *shows*. And that can be far worse than a defective heart.... No. You must consider the psychological effects of all these operations Wolf wants to do. And the pain associated with them. Roberts' solution might not be the ultimate but psychologically it might be the best." He leaned forward. "And you? How are you?" he asked. "You're looking just as beautiful as I remember."

"I'm all right. But I did lose a baby last year at eighteen weeks into the pregnancy."

"Do you know why?"

"A calf butted me in the stomach. And since there was no anesthesiologist available, the doctor had to do the D and C without anesthesia. Not once but twice. I was pretty much butchered up and almost died from the fever."

He winced and sat back staring silently at her for a few moments, his face grim. "Sounds to me like it's about time you got out of there," he said.

Diana decided on Roberts. He scheduled a preliminary examination at the Institute with his team of plastic surgeons and related specialists. Many came from other countries who were there to learn from the master. At the conclusion of the visit, Roberts started dictating a letter to his secretary who followed him about. It was addressed to Andrews' friend in Buenos Aires.

"No. No." Diana interrupted him. "I came here for the best. If I wanted to have your student do it, I wouldn't have come. I am not Argentine. I am a New Yorker," she stammered in front of the entire group of doctors. "I won't settle for second best for my son."

Roberts was startled. "Oh, I assumed that when you mentioned your doctor in Argentina, you had just come for my advice. But if

it has a tin roof, and when it rains on the pampas, it generally rains very hard.

"'A tin roof!' She was so shocked it was funny. 'You mean like in a barn? With no ceilings?'

"'It's called a casco,' I told her.

"She said no more because Philip returned, thrilled that she was right. Indeed, the attic here is the place where one can hear the rain."

Then, *"P.S. He's desperately trying to understand how television works."*

Later, Diana told her mother, "My casco is haunted, too," she laughed. "Several times I have seen the face of a gaucho who was killed there. He was watching me as I looked in my bathroom mirror, of all places!"

Her mother was silent for a while. Thinking. Troubled. Then she decided: "It's someone of your husband's family. His father?"

"Oh, no!"

"Do you know him? You've never mentioned him, nor his mother."

"His father committed suicide after his wife left him. And she died in the French Underground during the war. But it was neither one of them. It was a gaucho."

"Ghosts can take any form they want."

Despite Philip's fascination with the world of New York, Diana learned that he missed his father. When reading him his latest letter before putting him to sleep, tears came into his eyes. He turned away from her, faced the wall and wouldn't kiss her good night.

"I want to go back to Argentina," he murmured.

"We will someday."

"No." He turned to face her. "Now. I want to go back *now*. Right now. I want to see Papá. My Papá." And he started to cry.

Diana held him in her arms until he had cried himself to sleep, all the while aware that her resolute heart had just cracked and broken apart. Whatever doubts she had had about returning to Argentina vanished with her son's pleas.

Amazing. Roberts did the usual two-stage operation in one. If all goes well, we will be able to separate the lips in ten days."

She waited. And waited. Not daring to move, even to get a cup of coffee. At eleven-thirty P.M. a Dr. Mille from Belgium came to sit beside her. "He won't wake up, Madame. I think you might be able to help. If you promise not to faint, I'll take you up to the recovery room. Normally speaking, we never let mothers in the recovery room. They always faint. But from what I've heard about you in Argentina, I suspect you're stronger than most. He should have woken up long ago. Perhaps he will wake up for you."

"I promise not to faint." She followed him up to the eighth floor in the elevator, not exactly sure what he was talking about. She found out, though, as soon as she saw Philip. His arms and legs were strapped down like a martyr on a wheel of torture. Tubes stuck in him as though his life was being sucked out. His mouth had indeed been sewed together. Roberts had taken three fourths of his bottom lip, twisted it around and sewed it to the little bit of flesh under his nose to create the upper lip he had been born without.

His face was as gray white as the froth of a wild sea. "Philip," she called softly into his good ear. His eyes snapped open at the sound of her voice. Like lightning they struck into the depths of her—bulging with a terrifying kind of hatred. Wide with horror. She had betrayed him.

One of the two nurses standing close by told the other, "She didn't warn him his lips would be sewn together."

Diana turned on them. "But they didn't tell me it would be done now," she wept quietly, at all costs making Herculean efforts not to faint. She would not faint.

Diana took Philip's strapped-down hand and repeated over and over, "I love you," as he continued to glare at her, hating her for the abominable pain he was suffering and about which he was unable to utter a sound or make a sign of protest. Except with his big silver-gray eyes.

They put him in a special room with a fog machine, which kept the air laden with moisture. This, she was told, was for easy breathing and to prevent the stitches on his mouth from contracting. The water produced from this machine ran down the walls and dripped from the ceiling. She had to put on a raincoat to sit with him, and his bed had to be changed every hour.

She arrived at six A.M. every day and left after he had finally

operating room, Dr. Mille told her, "Keep your fingers crossed that the graft has taken. We can never be sure that the blood will continue to flow through the graft once the connection has been severed. If it does not, the graft turns black and dies, and all is lost."

Diana prayed. Her mother, too, would go to Mass in Watch Hill.

"For a moment there we weren't so sure, Madame," Dr. Mille announced to her five hours later, "but it worked. He will be just fine."

Philip became even more desperate to escape. He begged Diana to take him home to Argentina *now*. "Right *now*."

The day following the second operation a nurse came to him with his daily penicillin shot. As soon as he saw her he became hysterical. She called for help to hold him down and told Diana to leave the room. "I'll handle this," she told her. "Mothers are useless in cases like this."

As they were holding him down, Diana warned, "Be careful. He's very strong. Thin, but very strong. He's been raised on the pampas of Argentina."

Once again, the nurse ordered her out. But Diana ignored her, begging Philip to let the nurse do her job. As the nurse was bending over him, about to stick him, he managed to free one arm from the grip of another nurse, reached up and grabbed the dangling earring of the nurse who had her needle poised, ready to strike. He pulled it out of her ear, ripping right through the lobe. She fled, holding her ear dripping with blood. After that the nurses came armed with three male aides to hold him down.

Diana wrote to Michael, *"Philip's upper lip looks a bit pouting now. They've moved it forward a great deal, but under the nose it's still sunken, and I can't say it looks like a normal lip. As they told me, don't expect miracles. But really it's 1,000 percent better than it was. He's quite changed, and I'm feeling rather strange. Perhaps I'm just totally rung out emotionally. But it's hard for me to adjust. For me, his mother, who has lived with him for so long as he was—flesh of my flesh—and then to see this flesh changed.... Don't get me wrong. He's still our Philip. For the moment I just want to cry oceans of tears. I've been looking forward to this for so long and secretly hoping for miracles. Now that it is almost over, and I see that he is still not perfect, I feel this letdown.*

"The doctor said Philip might be able to go home on Tuesday. We will probably have to come back to thin out the section of flesh between the nos-

much whenever we got together...."

He never mentioned the Duchess.

Diana's mother called her when she heard her come in from the garden. She was upstairs in her bedroom, lying down, fully dressed, her face turned to the wall.

"You want to go back, don't you?"" she asked, continuing to stare at the wall.

"I have to, Mother."

"I know it."

Even when Diana sat down on the bed, her mother still did not turn to face her. "Well then, go to the travel agency in town and order tickets for yourself and Philip. Tell them to bill me. They will. They know me."

"But I still have to pay you back for the hospital. I'm looking for a job—"

"I know. But I couldn't stand seeing you like this anymore. Every day moping around. This man, whoever he is, whatever he is, needs you. I will accept the things you left here when you went to London in payment."

"When do you want me to leave?"

"Now, if you want. Any time."

"Oh, God, thank you, Mother." Diana reached over and gently touched her shoulder. She still did not move. At the threshold, Diana looked back at her. Only then did she turn over and smile.

Philip was joyous with the news that he would soon see his Papá. He exploded with such happiness that he ran outside and around the house several times as though to share the news with the entire world. When he came bursting back in again, he first looked at his grandmother, his eyes questioning, pleading. She knew right away what he wanted to ask.

"Yes. You may take the trains with you," she chuckled. "I don't know how they will work down there with your kind of electricity, but I'm sure your father will figure that out. If anyone can do so, he can. A man like him...."

"Strange," she softly smiled. "I never noticed how strong the smell was before." The odor of manure from the corral filled the air. "It must be the heaviness of the night."

"Yes. There is no wind."

The living room appeared narrow and dark, the cement walls cold and primitive, the fireplace obviously the work of an amateur builder. How could she have ever wanted so desperately to return to this?

"You see...." Michael welcomed her. "I have kept a fire going for you! And there is a stew on the stove. I made it myself and it's delicious. If you are hungry...."

But they weren't. Philip disappeared quickly into his room to make sure everything was as he had left it. After the boy had fallen asleep in his own bed, Diana lay stiffly next to Michael. They made love like strangers.

But all looked different in the morning. The sun poured into the living room, warming everything. Diana opened a window, and the sweet eastern breeze, smelling of earth and grass, stirred the white voile curtains, causing them to flutter gently like the wings of an angel hovering over a field of wildflowers. The color of the cement wall opposite turned a rich blue-gray. The yellow, comfortable, kapok-stuffed couch that Michael had made her when they were first married shone like the gold of the sunflower, and the dark green easy chairs flanking the fireplace like its leaves, sparkling as the dew-covered grass outside. The emerald satin lamp shades on the cut crystal lamps basked in the generous and warm morning light, reflecting sunshine into all corners of the room. The hum of the generator was comforting, not jarring and abusive to the ear as it had been the night before. Michael was already out milking the cows with his son, and Diana went into her kitchen to prepare breakfast for them.

After delivering the milk to the cheese factory, Michael and Philip came in to enjoy their favorite breakfast of warm French rolls spread with thick layers of butter, sweet white creamy cheese fresh from the factory, *dulce de leche* for Philip, and a pot of Diana's last year's marmalade made with their own oranges and mandarins.

"I forgot to tell you last night that Ernesto has left the Tres Marías for good," Michael told Diana, nonchalantly, not even bothering to look up from his coffee cup.

"Really?"

Michael, however, became increasingly silent and glum with each passing day. Few things Diana said or did seemed to please him. They began to argue again, spontaneously at first, and then bitterly.

When the Duchess came to visit, she barely acknowledged Diana as she jumped down from the cabin of her Dodge pickup. Her face bore its familiar haughty expression, as cold and noncommittal as an empty plate, and her hair was hidden, as usual, under her wool cap.

"So. You are back," she briefly declared. This time she was accompanied by her husband, the Duke. "He must have heard you were back," Michael murmured to Diana as he strode across the lawn to kiss her hand.

While Diana prepared coffee, the Duchess spoke to Michael about how and when they could start up again on her dairy now that his wife had returned and could help with the chores. Her machinery had just arrived in Customs. Michael was flattered, but evasive.

As they spoke the Duke set down the briefcase he was carrying on the table and announced to Diana, "I have come to do your horoscopes. Would you like that?"

"Wonderful!"

"All I need is the time and date of your births. Yours and Michael's."

"And Philips?"

"I don't do children that young. They haven't lived long enough."

"Fine. Michael," she interrupted the Duchess, "what exactly was the hour you were born? Do you know?"

"They tell me around one A.M."

"Then that would be November 25, 1927, for him. And nine P.M. March 31, 1933, for me," Diana told him, and the Duke noted this information carefully on a paper he withdrew from his briefcase.

"Now I just need a quiet place where I can work."

Diana led him to Michael's study, where he took out several charts from his briefcase and unfolded them on the desk. "And please close the door," he insisted sharply, sitting down, his eyes intently examining the papers before him.

When Diana returned to the living room the Duchess, with her back half-turned to Diana, took off her wool cap. Long and shiny

wrapped me in a poncho of some kind from Argentina, and she rubbed and rubbed my body with it until—it was twenty minutes they told me—before I began to move. To breathe. At that point the horse doctor turned away from my mother and devoted his attention to me. How about that! The good old Duke is right! I *was* born dead."

Several days later Diana passed the Duchess' Dodge speeding out of the campo as she turned into her road after a trip to Las Rosas. The Duchess' long blonde hair had been freed from her wool cap and was flying in the wind. Her eyes unseeing as she passed Diana. Her mouth grim.

She asked no explanations of Michael and he offered none.

The following day he announced he had to leave for San Juan. He returned by two P.M., just before Diana was about to take her siesta. He strode into the bedroom. "You are early," she said. "What happened?"

"We are wasting our time here."

"What do you mean?"

"We do not really belong here. It is finished."

"I could never leave."

"Don't lie," he accused her. "I shall never forget the look on your face the night I brought you back here from Rosario."

"It was just a question of getting adjusted—"

"No. It was more than that. You were shocked. You tried not to show it for my sake, I know. But you looked at me as though you didn't know me. And there was such *pity* in your eyes."

"Oh, no! It was gratitude that you saw. Gratitude that you had kept on for me. That you loved me.... It's the Duchess, isn't it?"

"Don't be a fool."

"She's in love with you."

"That doesn't mean I'm sleeping with her. And even if I were, I wouldn't admit it. The truth is I cannot let you continue to work like this. There is no more reason for it. I have accomplished what I set out to do. More or less. I can't do any more. Not in this country, I can't. Not with the kind of government it has."

"Perón will soon be back."

"Oh! Just you wait and see then. What a bordello this place will become. There will be a massacre. The military will let him in, sure. Tell the people he will fix everything. Just as he and Evita did back in the late 'forties. But *this* time he will be controlled by *them*.

about the countryside, looking for her mate, for her lost home in the monte? Would she become like Lucía, crying for her pampas far away?

"I'll talk to Rossio," Michael announced in the morning.

"Rossio?"

"Yes. Who else? No one else has the money, and as he said himself, anyone who does wouldn't want this place. You see, we could *rent* it to him as a showplace for his farm equipment, his stalls, and he could use our machine until his own are ready for sale."

She looked at him as though he had just proposed selling her soul to the devil. "*Rent*, I said. Not sell. But we would still have to sell some of our equipment and cattle to finance our trip."

"I don't want an auction here. I couldn't stand that."

"Nor could I. Don't worry. It won't be necessary," he assured her.

On Sunday Diana decided to take Philip to Mass. Michael accompanied them and stood next to her, holding her hand. The only other people present in the dark cathedral were old women—heads covered with black shawls and bent in prayerful silence while their men folk waited for them in the sunshine outside.

Diana noticed that Marta, along with Eric, was among the women. She waited for Diana outside the church after Mass, smiling radiantly as she told her about her new job. "I am so happy. And Eric is doing very well in school, and Mama loves it. She loves to fuss over him. And when I get home on weekends, we have a good time together. I have a nice little apartment now. Really, you should come and visit me."

"Thank you." Diana observed how well Eric conversed in Spanish with Philip. She wondered how Marta would feel when she learned that it would shortly be her turn to return to her native country.

"Soon, " Marta continued, "perhaps I shall have Eric come and live with me. But for now, anyway, he is much better off with his grandmother."

They met many friends outside the church, yet could not bear to tell anyone of their decision to leave. They spent the next month in furtive preparation for their departure. Diana only went into Las Rosas when she could not avoid it. She spoke to no one and kept her eyes averted from the questioning glances the villagers and her

MICHAEL came in after the cattle had gone and slumped down next to the fireplace. The optimism that had kept the light shining for so long in his eyes was extinguished, replaced by melancholy. Diana felt guilty that she had been thinking only of her own loss and served him a brandy. After taking one herself, she became lighthearted enough to exhort him: "Smile, *please*. Don't you see? We are free now. No more having to get up at four A.M. to milk cows. Just think! You can sleep till noon if you want to. No more worrying if the generator will start or not. Or the pickup. No more lugging drums of diesel, cylinders of propane. No more burning summers under this roof. Or being cooked to death out in the fields.

"Or lugging wood in the winter and huddling under blankets in a cold bed, in a freezing room, with icy water dripping from the ceiling onto your face. No more beetles attacking you in the summer as you try to milk at night after plowing all day. No more putting up with Mora and her antics. No more muddy roads. Or storms or hail to break your heart. No more barbed wire to cut your hands to pieces on. Don't you see?"

"Of course." He managed a weak smile for her.

"I've decided that we shall only take what we need with us. We shall leave our furnishings here. Leave everything as it is, so we shall have a home to come back to when we can. Right?"

"What about Alex? We can take him with us, if you wish."

"No.... Never. He belongs here. I would not dare do that to him. He would die within a few weeks in the city. In an apartment? He won't even get into a car, never mind a box on a plane. I will speak to Rosa Berrato. She will take care of him. No. He must stay here. Keeping watch. It is his home. In the winter he can keep warm in the machine room. And, to make sure he gets enough to eat, I will leave Rosa enough money to pay for food for a year."

They did not tell anyone but Rossio exactly when they planned to leave so they would have to say good-bye to no one. The day before their departure an old wagon rumbled up the road and stopped not far from the ombú. A young woman got down, holding a baby in her arms, followed by two little children. She walked determinedly over to the house and introduced herself to Michael. Her

"Come!" Michael called to her.

"It's all right." She returned slowly to the pickup, her eyes on the ombú, a voice far off reminding her that tragedy comes to the house upon whose shadow the ombú falls. She touched Michael's hand. "I'm all right," she murmured, as he sped off toward the high road as fast as he could.

"Good!"

He did not look back. But she did. And so did Philip. What they saw was the white mare galloping across the fields towards the glowing ombú that was now silhouetted against the western sky in the last light of the dying day.